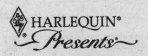

Lynne Graham

RELUCTANT MISTRESS, BLACKMAILED WIFE

GREEK
TYCOONS

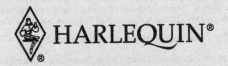

HARLEQUIN®

TORONTO • NEW YORK • LONDON
AMSTERDAM • PARIS • SYDNEY • HAMBURG
STOCKHOLM • ATHENS • TOKYO • MILAN • MADRID
PRAGUE • WARSAW • BUDAPEST • AUCKLAND

ISBN-13: 978-0-373-12580-7
ISBN-10:   0-373-12580-1

RELUCTANT MISTRESS, BLACKMAILED WIFE

First North American Publication 2006.

All about the author…
Lynne Graham

Born of Irish/Scottish parentage, **LYNNE GRAHAM** has lived in Northern Ireland all her life. She and her brother grew up in a seaside village. She now lives in a country house surrounded by a woodland garden, which is wonderfully private.

Lynne first met her husband when she was fourteen. They married after she completed her degree at Edinburgh University. Lynne wrote her first book at fifteen and it was rejected everywhere. She started writing again when she was at home with her first child. It took several attempts before she sold her first book and the delight of seeing that first book for sale in the local store has never been forgotten.

Lynne always wanted a large family and has five children. Her eldest, and only natural, child is in her twenties and a university graduate. Her other children, who are every bit as dear to her heart, are adopted: two from Sri Lanka and two from Guatemala. In Lynne's home, there is a rich and diverse cultural mix, which adds a whole extra dimension of interest and discovery to family life.

The family has two pets: Thomas, a very large and affectionate black cat, and Daisy, an adorable but not very bright white West Highland terrier, who loves being chased by the cat. At night, dog and cat sleep together in front of the kitchen stove.

Lynne loves gardening, cooking, collecting everything from old toys to rock specimens and is crazy about every aspect of Christmas.

CHAPTER ONE

As WRY amusement lit his eyes, which could be as dark and deep as an underground river, Alexandros Christakis watched his grandfather walk round the sleek silver Ascari KZ1 he had just had delivered. A supercar, it was the ultimate boy-toy, for only fifty would ever be built. The older man's excitement at being that close to such a rare and powerful vehicle was palpable.

'A car that costs almost a quarter of a million.' Pelias, tall and straight in spite of his seventy-five years, shook his grizzled head and smiled with almost boyish approval. 'It is sheer madness, but it does my heart good to see you taking an interest in such things again!'

Alexandros said nothing in response to that leading comment, his expression unrevealing, his legendary reserve impenetrable. Gossip columnists regularly referred to the billionaire head of the CTK Bank as beautiful. Alexandros loathed the press, and had little time for such frivolity. His lean, bronzed features might have a breath-taking symmetry that turned female heads wherever he went, but the forceful angle of his jawline, the tough slant of his cheekbones and the obdurate set of his wide, sensual mouth suggested a fierce strength of character that was more of a warning to the unwary.

'You're still a young man—only thirty-one years old.' Pelias Christakis spoke with caution, for he had long been in awe of his brilliant grandson and rarely dared breach his reticence. 'Naturally I understand that you will never forget your grief, but it is time for you to take up your life once more.'

Marvelling at the old man's essential innocence, Alexandros murmured flatly, 'I took my life back a long time ago.'

'But all you have done since Ianthe passed away is work, and make more and more money from bigger and bigger deals! How much money can one man need in a lifetime? How many homes can one man use?' Pelias Christakis flung up his hands in an extrovert gesture that encompassed the superb Regency country house in front of him. And Dove Hall was only one item in his grandson's vast property portfolio. 'You are already rich beyond most men's dreams.'

'I thought onwards and upwards was the Christakis motto.' Alexandros brooded on the unhappy truth that people were never satisfied. He had been raised to be an Alpha-male high-achiever, with the merciless killer instincts of a shark. He was competitive, ambitious, and aggressive when challenged. Every aspect of his upbringing had been carefully tailored to ensure that he grew up as the exact opposite of his late father, who had been a lifelong layabout and an embarrassment to his family.

'I'm proud of you—immensely proud,' his grandfather hastened to assert in an apologetic undertone. 'But the world can offer you so much more than the next takeover or merger. Companionship may seem an old-fashioned concept—'

'Of course there have been women.' Alexandros compressed his handsome mouth, only his respect for the older man's good intentions restraining him from the delivery of a more caustic response. 'Is that what you want to hear?'

Pelias raised a beetling brow in rueful emphasis. 'I'll be more interested to hear that you've been with the same woman for longer than a week!'

Exasperated by that censorious response, Alexandros immediately grasped what his grandfather was driving at, and cold annoyance overpowered tolerance. 'But I'm not in the market for anything serious. I have no intention of getting married again.'

His companion treated him to a look of surprise. 'Did I mention marriage?'

Unimpressed by that air of virtuous naivety—for Pelias was not a good dissembler—Alexandros said nothing. He was grimly aware that the very fact that he was an only child put an extra weight of expectation and responsibility on him. Traditional Greek culture set great store on the carrying on of the family name. Understandably, his grandparents held the convictions of their age group. But Alexandros felt equally entitled to his own views, and believed that only honesty would suffice. As he had not the slightest desire to be a father, he had no plans to remarry. Becoming a parent had been his late wife's dream, if not her obsession. Now that Ianthe was gone, he saw no reason to pretend otherwise.

'I don't want another wife...or children, for that matter,' Alexandros admitted in a flat, unapologetic undertone, his lean dark face aloof. 'I appreciate that this must disappoint you, but that's how it is and I'm not going to change.'

Pelias Christakis had lost colour. Stripped of all the natural exuberance of his warm, engaging personality, he suddenly looked old, troubled, and very much at a loss. Feeling like the guy who had not only killed but also tortured Santa Claus, Alexandros suppressed any urge to soften the blow and raise false hopes. It had had to be said.

* * *

Now a veteran at jumble sales, Katie leapt straight into the competitive fray, rummaging through the pile of baby clothes. Emerging victorious with an incredibly smart little jacket and trouser set, she asked the lady on the stall, 'How much for this?'

It was more than she could afford, and she put it back with a regret that was only fleeting—because she had long since learned that her real priorities were shelter, food and warmth. Clothes came fourth on her survival list of necessities, so newness and smartness were almost always out of reach. She found a sweater and a pair of jeans at a price within her means. Though both garments were shabby they had plenty of life left in them. The twins were growing so fast that keeping them clothed was a constant challenge. As she paid, the lady offered to reduce the price on the trouser set, but Katie flushed and said no thanks, for she had now spent what she had to spare. The pity she saw in the woman's eyes embarrassed her.

'They're lovely boys,' the stallholder said reluctantly. She had noticed that Katie's hands were bare of rings, and although she hoped she was a charitable woman she very much disapproved of young unwed mothers.

Katie glanced at her sons, seated side by side in the worn twin buggy, and a rueful smile of maternal pride crept across the weary line of her mouth. Toby and Connor were gorgeous babies, and very well advanced for their age of nine months. The combination of black curly hair, pale golden skin and big brown eyes gave them an angelic air that was rather deceptive. The twins thrived on attention and activity, screeched the place down when disappointed, whinged at length when bored, and required very little sleep. But Katie absolutely adored them, and often studied them with the dazed feeling that she could not possibly have given birth to two such clever and beautiful children. Not only did they not look like her, they did not act like her either. Only in low moments, when she was fighting total exhaustion, was she willing to admit that she was finding it a real struggle to cope with their constant demands.

On the walk home, she found herself looking at other young women. It bothered her when she caught herself thinking that the ones without kids seemed more youthful, light-hearted and attractive. She saw her reflection in a shop window and stared, her heart sinking. Suddenly she wanted to cry. There had been a time when, had she made the required effort, she would have been called pretty. Now that was just a memory, and she was a small thin girl with a pinched face and red hair caught back in a ponytail. She looked nondescript and plain. She swallowed hard, knowing that Toby and Connor's father would never look at her now.

Once she had marvelled that he had ever deigned to notice her. She had thought it was so romantic that a dazzlingly attractive male who could have had literally any woman should instead have chosen her. But the passage of time and cruel experience had destroyed her fanciful illusions one by one and forced her to face less palatable truths. Now Katie accepted that he had only noticed her because she had been the sole female in his vicinity when he'd felt like sex. She had given him what he wanted without making a single demand. He had never at any stage regarded her as anything other than a social inferior—for he had never even taken her out on a date. When her breathless adoration had palled, he had dumped her so hard and fast she still shivered thinking about it. Nothing had ever hurt her as much as that cold, harsh descent from fantasy to reality.

Only a few minutes after she'd got back to her bedsit, her landlord appeared at her door. 'You'll have to go,' he told her bluntly. 'I've had another complaint about the noise your kids make at night.'

Katie stared at him in horror. 'But all babies cry—'

'And two babies make twice as much of a din.'

'I swear I'll try to keep them quieter—'

'You said that the last time I spoke to you, and nothing's changed,' the older man cut in, unimpressed. 'You've had your warning and I'm giving you two weeks' notice. If you don't move out willingly, I'll have you evicted. So let's keep it simple. Get yourself down to Social Services and they'll soon sort you out with another place!'

Appalled at his belligerent attitude, Katie tried in vain to reason with him. Long after he had gone, she sat with her arms wrapped round herself while she fought the awful feeling of despair stealing over her. She was painfully aware that she had virtually no hope of fighting such a decree when complaints had been lodged against her. Her tenancy was only of the unassured variety, and she did not even feel she could blame the other tenants for kicking up a fuss. The walls were paper-thin and the twins did regularly cry at night.

The bedsit needed decorating, the furniture was battered and the shared facilities were dismal. But the room had still come to feel like home to Katie. Furthermore, the building was in good repair and the area was reasonably respectable and safe. She was not afraid to walk down the street. Unlike during her pregnancy, when she had spent a couple of months in a flat on an inner city estate. Drug dealing and gang warfare had been a way of life there, and she had been terrified every time she'd had to go out.

Although she had been about to put Toby and Connor

down for a nap, she realised that she would have to go straight back out again. In two short weeks she would be homeless, and she needed to give the housing authorities as much time as possible to locate alternative accommodation for them. Just when had she sunk so low that she no longer had the power to help herself? She blinked back a sudden rush of tears. She was twenty-three years old. She had always been a doer—independent, energetic and industrious. But she had not realised how difficult it would be to raise two children alone. She had not realised how poor she would be either. Indeed, in the latter stages of pregnancy she had made enthusiastic plans about getting her career back on track. She had expected to return to full-time employment, not end up dependent on welfare handouts for survival. Ill-health, accommodation problems, transport costs and sleepless nights had slowly but surely destroyed her hopes.

A week crawled past, during which Katie did everything she could to find somewhere else to live. But the few leads she had got turned into dead ends. Midway through the second week she began to panic, and a social worker informed her that she would have to go into emergency bed and breakfast accommodation.

'You'll hate it,' her friend Leanne Carson declared. 'The room won't be yours to do what you want with, and there probably won't be any cooking facilities.'

'I know,' Katie muttered heavily.

'Crying babies won't be flavour of the month there either.' The pretty blue-eyed brunette whom Katie had met in hospital sighed, 'You'll be moved on again in no time. Why are you being such a doormat?'

'What do you mean?'

'You told me that the twins' dad had money. Why don't

you spread a little of that cash in your own direction? If the stingy creep is newsworthy and wealthy enough, you could sell your story to the press.'

'Don't be daft.' Katie pressed pale fingers to her pounding temples.

'Of course you'd have to spice the story up. Ten-times-a-night sex, how insatiable or kinky his demands were—you know the sort of thing…'

Katie reddened to the roots of her hair. 'No, I don't—'

'The sordid details are what make tittle-tattle like that entertaining and worth oodles of cash. Don't be such a prude! The guy's a total bastard. He deserves to be embarrassed!'

'Maybe he does, but I couldn't do it. That's not what I'm about. I appreciate that you're only trying to help, but—'

'You're never going to get up out of the gutter with that bad attitude.' Leanne rolled scornful eyes heavy with mascara and glittering blue shadow. 'Are you just going to lie down and die? Let the bloke get away with it? If you really love your little boys, you'll be ready to do whatever it takes to give them a better life!'

Katie flinched as though she had been slapped.

Leanne dealt her a defiant look. 'It's true, and you know it is. You're letting the kids' father…this Alexandros whatever…you're letting him escape his responsibilities.'

'I contacted the Child Support Agency—'

'Yeah, like they've got the time and resources to try and pin your kids on some foreign business tycoon! He's rich. He'd refuse to take DNA tests, or he'd stay out of the country, or pretend he'd lost all his money. If you insist on playing it by the book, you'll never see a penny from him,' the other woman forecast with cynical conviction. 'No, if you ask me, you're only going to escape your current problems if you do a kiss-and-tell for the tabloids!'

Katie couldn't sleep that night. She thought of the sacrifices her own mother had had to make to bring her up. Widowed when her daughter was only six, Maura had had to work as a cleaner, a caretaker and a cook to make ends meet. In the darkness, Katie lay still and taut with discomfiture. Alexandros had dumped her, ignored her appeal for help and broken her stupid heart. She had decided she would sooner starve than appeal to him again. But had she let false pride get in the way of her duty towards her infant sons? Was Leanne right? Could she have done more to press her case with Alexandros?

Two days later, Katie moved out of her bedsit with Leanne's help. Luckily her friend was able to store some stuff for her. The surplus had to be dumped or passed on to be sold on a market stall, because Katie could not afford storage costs. The bed and breakfast hotel was crowded and her room was small, drab and depressing.

After spending her first night there, Katie rose heavy-eyed, but driven by a new and fierce determination. She had decided that she was willing to do whatever it took to give Toby and Connor a secure roof over their heads. The prospect of public embarrassment and humiliation and further rejection should not deter her. Right now she was letting her kids down by acting like a wimp, she told herself squarely. Leanne had been right to speak up. More vigorous action was definitely required.

With that in mind, Katie went to the library to use the internet and see if she could discover any new information about Alexandros. She had tried and failed several times before, and quite a few months had passed since her last effort. But this time the search offered her the option of trying an alternative name, and when she tried that link she stared in shock as the screen filled with potential sites. A recognisable photo of Alexandros folded down on the very first she visited.

It only then dawned on Katie that her previous searches had been unsuccessful because she had spelled his name as Crestakis, *not* Christakis. She had got his name wrong. She was stunned. That crucial yet simple mistake had ensured that she hadn't found out that Alexandros was the chief executive of CTK Bank, which had a substantial office in London. All the time that she had been engaged in a desperate struggle for survival, Alexandros had been making regular trips to the UK!

For a while she just surfed, seeing him variously described as brilliant, beautiful, arctic-cool, impassive. This was the guy she had fallen crazily in love with, all right, although she had refused to accept back then that she was on a highway to nowhere. The nape of her neck prickled when she read a newspaper report about a merger announcement expected from CTK the next morning. If something big was in the air, Alexandros was almost certain to be putting in an appearance. If she got up early, she could go to the City, wait outside the bank, and try to intercept him when he arrived.

Of course she could also go the more normal route and ask for an appointment with him, couldn't she? Her soft mouth down-curved at that idea. She was convinced that he wouldn't agree to see her. After all, he had given her a useless phone number on which to contact him at their final meeting, and had also ignored her letter asking for his help. No, perhaps it would be wiser not to forewarn Alexandros. An element of surprise might just give her the edge she badly needed; she was no longer naive enough to believe that she could easily hold her own with someone that clever and callous.

Katie left the twins with Leanne at a very early hour the next day.

'Now, don't you take any nonsense off this guy,' her friend warned her anxiously. 'He's got more to lose than you have.'

'How do you make that out?' Katie lowered Toby and then Connor into the playpen already occupied by Leanne's daughter, Sugar. As always, she was looking around herself and wishing she was in a position to afford similar accommodation. Although her friend's home was tiny, the rainbow pastels she favoured made the rooms feel bright and welcoming even on a dull day. Helped by a family support network that Katie lacked, Leanne worked as a hairdresser. Her mother often looked after her grandchild in the evenings, and her ex-boyfriend paid maintenance.

'I bet you anything he won't want a scandal,' Leanne declared. 'According to what I've read, bankers are supposed to be a very conservative bunch…anything else makes the punters nervous!'

Conservative? That adjective danced around in the back of Katie's mind when she was on the bus. On first acquaintance, Alexandros *had* struck her as conservative—indeed, icily reserved and austere. She hadn't liked him, hadn't liked being treated like a servant, and had hated the innate habit of command that was so much a part of his bred-in-the-bone arrogant assurance. But not one of those facts had snuffed out the wicked longing he had stirred up inside her. Her response to him had shocked her, and shattered all her neat, bloodless little assumptions about her own nature. His sizzling passion had shocked her even more. He had just grabbed her up and kissed her, and then carried her off to bed without hesitation or discussion. She cringed at that recollection, which she rarely let out of her memory-bank. She had acted like a slut and—not surprisingly, in her opinion—he had treated her like one.

CTK Bank was situated in the heart of the City of London, an impressive contemporary edifice with a logo hip enough to front a top fashion brand. She stared up at the light-reflecting gleam of ranks of windows, marvelling at the sheer size and splendour of the office block. Anger flared through her nervous tension, making her restless. Alexandros Christakis was, she finally appreciated, a very wealthy and powerful man. She positioned herself at the corner of the building so that she could watch both the front and the side entrances. Employees were starting to arrive. Rain came on steadily, quickly penetrating the light jacket she wore and drenching her. With her head bent to avoid the downpour, she almost missed the big car purring to a discreet halt in the quiet side street.

Straightening with a jerk, she began to walk very fast towards the limo—if the VIP passenger was Alexandros she didn't want to miss him. Two other cars had also pulled up—one to the front of the luxury vehicle, the second to the rear. Several men emerged and fanned out across the street. Katie's scrutiny, however, was glued to the tall dark male descending from the limousine. The breeze ruffled his luxuriant ebony hair. Without warning, a painful sense of familiarity, sharp as a knife-blade, pierced Katie. She would have known him anywhere just by the angle of his imperious head and the economic grace with which he moved. The chill of sudden shocked recognition engulfed her. Her attention locked to his lean, powerful face, marking the straight slash of his black brows, the dark, deep-set allure of his brilliant gaze. Her tummy flipped and she was dazzled.

'Alexandros…' She tried to speak but her voice failed her.

Because even though he could not have heard her, for she was still too far away, he did seem to be looking her way.

Alexandros had picked up on the alert stance of his security team and zeroed in on the source. But the instant he saw the small slender figure approaching him he knew her, and he was so surprised he stopped dead in his tracks. The wet gleam of her wine-red hair and her pale heart-shaped face struck a haunting chord that plunged him into an instant flashback. He remembered sunshine streaming through a rain-washed window over that amazing hair, lighting up eyes of an almost iridescent green. It had been a stark moment of truth in an interlude that he was reluctant to recall. One of his bodyguards blocked her path with practised ease, just as a posse of paparazzi came charging down the street behind her, waving cameras.

'Inside, boss,' Cyrus, his head of security urged as Alexandros hesitated. 'Paparazzi and a homeless kid... could be a set-up!'

In one long stride, Alexandros mounted the steps and vanished into the building. A set-up? A homeless kid? Cyrus could only have been referring to Katie. Why was she still dressing like a scruffy student? And *why* had she come to see him? He could not believe that her sudden appearance after so long would be a coincidence. What did she want from him? Why would she try to approach him in a public place? Had the paparazzi been waiting and watching to see if he acknowledged her, ready to spring some kind of a trap in which he was the target? Hard suspicion flaring in his shrewd gaze, he told Cyrus to watch Katie's every move.

It took a lot to surprise Cyrus, but that instruction achieved it.

'The female you assumed was a homeless kid? Her name is Katie Fletcher. Don't let your team lose her!' Alexandros warned in rapid Greek. 'Follow her. I want to know where she lives.'

As his efficient security chief hurried back outside to carry out his orders, Alexandros switched back into working mode. Stepping into the executive lift held in readiness for him, he was immediately immersed in a quote of the latest share prices and the final adjustments to the press release to be made about the merger. When another memory tried to surface from his usually disciplined subconscious, he rooted it out with ruthless exactitude. He was not introspective. He did not relive past mistakes. In fact he had long since accepted that on the emotional front he was as cold as his reputation.

At the end of his first meeting he discovered that he had printed a K and encircled it, and the knowledge of that brief loss of concentration, that subliminal weakness that had defied his control, infuriated him.

Taken aback by the blocking technique of the security man, who had got in her way, and then rudely crowded off the pavement by the heaving, shouting and disgruntled members of the press, who had surged past her in an effort to get at Alexandros, Katie was momentarily at a loss. Alexandros had seen her. But had he recognised her? Had he sent that beefy security guy to ward her off? Would he have spoken to her if the journalists had not been present?

She thought not. He hadn't smiled, hadn't shown the smallest sign that a friendly welcome might be in the offing. He was such a bastard, she thought painfully, a horrible sense of failure seeping through her. But even as her shoulders drooped, a defiant spirit of rebellion was powering her up again. She marched back round the corner and through the front doors of the bank, and right up to the reception desk.

'I'd like to speak to Mr Christakis,' she announced.

The receptionist who came to attend to her studied Katie fixedly, as if trying to decide whether or not she was pulling her leg. In that intervening moment of assessment Katie became uncomfortably aware of her sodden hair and shabby jacket and jeans.

'I'll take your name.' The elegant young woman behind the desk switched on her professional cool. 'But I should warn you that Mr Christakis is exceptionally busy and his appointments are usually booked months in advance. Perhaps you could see someone else?'

'I want to see Alexandros. Someone else won't do. Please just see that he gets my name. He knows me.' Aware of the silent disbelief which greeted that declaration, Katie retreated with as much dignity as she could manage to a seat. She watched the receptionist commune with her two colleagues. Someone stifled a giggle, and her anxious face burned as she affected an interest she did not feel in the heavy-duty financial publications laid out for perusal on a coffee table. She was getting paranoid, she scolded herself. In all probability nobody was talking about her—just as the most likely explanation for what had happened outside was that Alexandros simply hadn't recognised her.

She lifted an uncertain hand to her wet hair and suddenly reached round to undo her ponytail. She dug a comb out of her bag and surreptitiously began to tease out the limp damp curls, praying for her natural ringlets to emerge, rather than the pure frizz that had made her scrape her hair back so tightly when she was a teenager that her eyes had used to water. She wondered why she was bothering. He wouldn't agree to see her.

While she sat there she finally registered a fact that should have occurred to her sooner. She had got his name totally wrong. Had Alexandros ever even received her letter telling him that she was pregnant? She had sent one to his Irish residence, and when there had been no answer she had sent a second one care of the rental company that had leased the house to him. But would a letter with the wrong name on it have been forwarded? What if Alexandros hadn't got either?

'Miss Fletcher?' the receptionist murmured.

Katie stood up hurriedly. 'Yes?'

'I have a call for you.'

Surprise marking her delicate triangular features, Katie accepted the cordless phone extended to her.

'Katie?'

It was Alexandros, and she was so taken aback by the sound of that dark melodic drawl of his that she almost dropped the phone. 'Alexandros?'

'I'm waiting for a fix on a satellite link and I'm afraid that I only have a few minutes. You've picked a bad day to call…'

'The merger,' she filled in, the receiver crammed tight to her ear as she wandered away in a preoccupied daze. His voice had an aching familiarity that tugged cruelly at her heartstrings and threatened to take her back in time. 'But that's why I came. I knew you'd be here, and I have to see you.'

'Why?' Alexandros enquired with the most studious casualness. Everything she had so far said was setting off warning bells of caution. 'Do you need some sort of help? Is that why you asked to see me?'

'Yes…but it's not something I can discuss on the phone or without privacy,' Katie told him tautly. 'Just out of interest…er…did you ever receive a letter from me?'

'No.'

'Oh…' Katie was stumped by that unhesitating negative, for if he didn't even know that she had been pregnant he was in for a huge shock.

'Why can't you just tell me in brief what this is about?' Alexandros enquired drily.

'Because I *have* to see you to talk about it,' she reminded him, feeling under unfair pressure and not knowing how to deal with it in the circumstances.

'That may not be possible—'

Katie lowered her voice to say, almost pleadingly, 'I wouldn't have come here if I wasn't desperate—'

'Then cut to the chase,' he cut in with cold clarity. 'I'm not into mysteries.'

A surge of angry tears burned the back of Katie's eyes. 'Okay, so you won't see me,' she gasped. 'But don't say I didn't give you the chance!'

With that ringing declaration, Katie cut the connection and marched back to the desk to return the phone. Before she could even set it down it started ringing again, and as she walked away the receptionist called her name a second time. She spun round. The handset was being offered to her. She shook her head in urgent refusal. She was uneasily conscious that quite a few people seemed to be staring in her direction, particularly a thin fair man with sharp eyes that made her colour. Without further ado she turned on her heel and headed hurriedly out of the bank.

She was furious that she had been so impulsive and naive. It had been downright stupid to try and speak to Alexandros again! He didn't want to speak to her or hear from her, and the news that he was the father of twins would be even less welcome. She reckoned that the only way she was likely to get financial help from Alexandros now would be by approaching a solicitor to make a paternity claim. But she also knew that legal wheels turned very slowly, and would not provide an answer in the short term. So she needed to think about overcoming her scruples and approaching a newspaper, she conceded unhappily.

Alexandros would be very angry with her. A shard of all too vivid memory was assailing her. She remembered throwing a breakfast tray at him and screaming. His expression of shock would live with her to her dying day. It had dawned on her then that nobody had ever spoken to Alexandros like that before, or told him that he was absolute hell to work for and impossible to please. Her disrespect had affronted him. Only when he had been persuaded to see her side of things had he been willing to forgive the offence, and he had still ended up getting his own way. *My way or the highway* was a punchline that might have coined for Alexandros Christakis.

It took Katie an hour to get back to Leanne's flat, but nobody was in when she got there. Her friend had warned her that she might go shopping with her mother, she recalled ruefully. As she walked back along the street, a limousine nudged into the kerb just ahead of her, and a big middle-aged man in a suit leapt out to jerk open the passenger door.

'Mr Christakis would like to give you a lift,' he announced.

Taken by surprise, she froze, studying the tinted black windows of the long glossy silver vehicle with frowning intensity before moving forward in abrupt acceptance of the invitation. Whether she liked it or not, she knew that it was the best offer she was likely to get. Her heartbeat racing so fast that she felt dizzy, she climbed into the limo.

CHAPTER TWO

ALEXANDROS dealt Katie a grim nod of acknowledgement that would have made her shiver, had not less cautious responses already been running rampant within her.

Lounging back in a black designer suit teamed with a striped shirt and smooth silk tie, he was the very image of the billionaire banker she had read about on the internet. Handsome, incredibly sophisticated, and intimidating to the nth degree though that sleek image was, there was also something impossibly sexy about him. She went hot pink with shame at that perverse thought. He had not lost the power to reduce her principles and her common sense to rubble round her feet.

'If you wanted my attention, you've got it,' Alexandros delivered with lethal cool, while he appraised her, his keen scrutiny highly critical. She had the heart-shaped face of a cat, big eyes above slanted cheekbones and a generous mouth. Unusual, rather exotic, but ultimately nothing special, with a tangle of bright copper hair that cruelly accentuated the hollows and shadows in her pale features. She was tiny and fine-boned—too thin for his tastes. By no stretch of the imagination was she beautiful—and some of the most beautiful women in the world had adorned his bed. He could not imagine why she had once made him seethe with lust.

Her lashes lifted on languorous eyes as rich and deep a green as moss. His gaze instantly narrowed, increasing in intensity almost without his volition. She shifted position with an indescribably feline movement of slender limbs that made his big powerful frame tense.

The silence stretched and stretched.

'So…?' Alexandros prompted, his dark drawl rough-edged as he fought the raw tide of sensual memory afflicting him. She had always smelt of soap and fresh air. The most expensive perfume in the world made her sneeze uncontrollably. He cleared his mind of that frivolous imagery with the rigorous restraint that had been second nature to him from his early twenties. He had learned then how to shut down and shut out unwelcome emotions and reactions. He thought it significant that he had got involved with Katie Fletcher when he had been emotionally off balance. Presumably, and ironically, that had added an extra edge which his encounters had lacked since then.

'What's this about?' he asked with level austerity.

Just watching him, Katie felt her mouth run dry—because he was *so* incredibly handsome. She found herself tracing the image of her sons in his lean bronzed features, noting the straight dark brows, the definite chin and nose, and the ebony hair that gleamed with vitality. Her little boys were like mini-clones of their father. She lowered her lashes, discomfiture taking over, for what she had to tell him loomed over her like a mountain that shut out the sun. He would soon be wishing that he had never laid eyes on her, she thought painfully. 'I wish you'd got that letter I sent you…'

To Alexandros she looked so young at that moment that

guilt penetrated even his polished armour of self-containment. What lustful madness had overcome his scruples eighteen months ago? He might as well have seduced a schoolgirl. Every word she spoke underlined the reality that she had been defenceless. The other women he had known wouldn't write him letters after he dumped them.

'Let's move on from the letter.' Alexandros was now taking further note of her shabby clothes, and the fact that the sole was peeling off one of her trainers. Her poverty was obvious and his distrust increased. He could not forget the potential threat with which she had concluded their exchange on the phone. 'What's happened to you?'

Wretchedly aware of his visual inspection, and inwardly cringing from it, Katie muttered tightly, apologetically, 'I know…I don't look the same, do I? Life's been tough over the past year—'

'If you need money, I'll give it to you. Drama and sob stories are not required,' Alexandros imparted.

Her pointed chin came up in a defiant motion, her green eyes full of strain and hurt pride. 'My goodness, did you think I was about to make you sit through some sob story? Well, then, I won't try to wrap up the bad news. I'll just get to the point. You got me pregnant…'

Astonished by that claim, Alexandros went straight into defensive mode, not a muscle moving on his darkly handsome face.

Katie was as pale as milk. 'I wasn't very pleased either. Well, to be honest, I was just terrified—'

'Is this some kind of sting? It's a very clumsy one.'

Her white brow indented. 'A *sting*?' she repeated blankly.

'I don't believe that I made you pregnant. Why would I only be hearing about it now?' Alexandros demanded in a smooth, derisive undertone that suggested that what she had said was too stupid for words. 'How can you expect me to believe this nonsense?'

'The reason that you're only hearing about it now is that you didn't give me your address.'

'But I left you a phone number.'

'And I rang it more than a dozen times, and every time I was told you were unavailable or in a meeting!' Her voice rose as she recalled how her sense of humiliation had grown with every fruitless phone call.

Alexandros continued to look stonily unimpressed. 'I don't accept that. My staff are very efficient—'

'Eventually one of your employees got so tired of my calls that she took pity on me. She explained that I wasn't on the special list she had. And, as she said, "If your name isn't on my boss's list, you won't get to speak to him this side of eternity!"' Katie completed rawly.

Alexandros was frowning. 'Your name must have been on the list—'

'No, it wasn't. Why pretend? We both know why my name wasn't on your fancy VIP list,' Katie condemned, with a bitterness she could not hide. 'You didn't want to hear from me. You had no wish for further contact. That's fine, that's okay, but don't try and criticise me for not telling you I was pregnant when I had no way of contacting you!'

'You're hysterical…I'm not continuing this conversation with you,' Alexandros asserted with cold clarity, outrage turning his dark eyes into chips of gold ice because she had raised her voice.

Katie snatched in a deep, shuddering breath even as she wondered if he remembered her once serving him coffee on her knees to make him laugh. 'I'm not hysterical. I'm sorry I'm so angry, but I can't help it. I should've known this wasn't going to work. I shouldn't have come to your precious bank and I shouldn't have got into this car—'

'Calm down,' Alexandros interposed with chilling cool, while he tried to work out her motivation for the tale she was telling so badly. He could not credit that what she was telling him was true. He was willing to admit that with her he had not been one hundred per cent careful when it had come to contraception. There was a very slight possibility that conception could have taken place. He thought it highly unlikely, though, and his usually alert and versatile mind was curiously reluctant to move on from that concrete conviction. He did not recognise his own unresponsiveness as simple shock at the announcement she had made.

Katie put trembling hands up to her face and covered it. *Calm down?* Her brow was pounding hard with tension; her tummy was in twisting knots. As he watched her, his lean hands clenched but he remained otherwise motionless.

On the other side of the glass partition, Cyrus was trying to catch his employer's eye in the mirror, to work out where to go next. In a sudden decision, Alexandros touched a button to seal the passenger area into privacy. If she cried, he did not want her tears to be witnessed. 'It's all right,' he told her grittily, for gentleness did not come naturally to him and he would not let himself reach across the space separating them to make physical contact with her. 'You'll be fine.'

'Nothing's all right…' Katie felt as if she was banging her head up against a brick wall. He wasn't listening. He didn't believe her. She was wasting her breath. He would probably look at Toby and Connor and find it equally easy to say that they weren't his. Then what? She bowed her head, exhaustion overwhelming the nervous energy that had powered her into confronting him.

Alexandros recognised her fragile emotional state. She

was desperate and broke. Presumably that was why she had come to him with a foolish story that she had hoped would engage his sympathy. It must not have occurred to her that a fictional tale about a pregnancy that had come to nothing was pointless. But his anger had already ebbed, to be replaced by an effort to understand her predicament that would have disconcerted anyone who knew him well. While he gave freely to a host of worthy charitable causes, he had always avoided situations where anything more personal was required.

'Are you unemployed?' he asked, deciding to concentrate on practicalities in the hope that those issues would ground her.

Katie darted a surprised glance at him above her fingers and slowly, carefully, lowered her hands back down on to her lap. 'Yes.'

'So you decided to approach me for…help. That's okay.' Alexandros resolved to offer assistance in every way he could. 'Where are you living at present?'

Unsure where this dialogue could be heading, Katie blinked. 'In a bed and breakfast hotel…I had to leave the bedsit I was in.'

Alexandros had not a clue what a bed and breakfast hotel was. But he knew a bedsit was one room, which he found shocking enough in the accommodation stakes. He surveyed her, wondering if she had lost weight because she wasn't getting enough to eat. He was sincerely shaken by that thought. 'Are you hungry?'

Slowly, she nodded, for it was hours since she had eaten, but his questions were bewildering her. 'Aren't you going to ask me about the baby?'

The repetition of that unfortunate word 'baby' had the same effect on Alexandros as a bucket of cold water. His lean, strong face hardened. 'I thought we had moved on from that improbable tale. It's not winning you any points with me.'

Katie flushed a deep painful pink. 'Why are you so convinced that I'm lying? Do I have to go through a solicitor for you to take me seriously?'

Almost imperceptibly Alexandros tensed; that reference to legal counsel did not fit the conclusions he had reached.

'You just don't want to know, do you?' Katie shook her head in pained and angry embarrassment. 'But I'm bringing up your children!'

'My...*children*?' Alexandros repeated in blunt disbelief. 'Are you out of your mind?'

'I had twins... Have you any idea how hard this is for me?' Katie demanded chokily. 'How do you think it feels for me to have to ask you for a hand-out?'

Twins! That single word hit Alexandros harder than any other. It was a fact known to few that he was a twin, whose sibling had been stillborn. 'You're telling me that you have given birth to twins?'

'What do you care?' she gasped. 'Look, stop the car and let me out...I've had enough of this!'

'Give me your address.'

While Alexandros opened the shutter between them and the chauffeur and communicated in Greek, she clasped her hands tightly together to conceal the fact that she couldn't hold them steady.

Alexandros focussed bleak dark golden eyes on her. 'What age are the twins?'

It dawned on her that he was finally listening to her. 'Nearly ten months old.'

The improbable began to look ever more possible to Alexandros. Yet on another level he could not believe that he could find himself in such a situation. On every instinc-

tive level he resisted that belief. 'And you are saying that
your children are mine?'

There was no mistaking how appalled Alexandros
Christakis was by the idea that she might just be telling him
the truth after all, Katie registered with a sinking heart. His
vibrant skin tone had paled, and the stunned light in his
gorgeous dark eyes spoke for him. 'What else do you think
I'm doing here? Oh, right—you're still hoping it's a sting.
Sorry, I'm not a con-artist. The twins are yours and there's
no mistake about that.'

'I will insist on DNA tests,' Alexandros asserted.

Katie veiled her eyes, angrily reeling from that further
insult as though he had struck her. How dared he? He was
the only lover she had ever had, even if he had chosen not
to acknowledge the fact. The harsh bite of hurt and rejection lurked behind her annoyance, but she stubbornly
refused to acknowledge it. Never once since he'd walked
away from her had she allowed herself to wallow in the
pain of that loss.

Yet what more had she expected from Alexandros
Christakis today? she asked herself unhappily. Had she
dreamt of a welcome mat and immediate acceptance of her
announcement? From a guy who had ditched her while
carefully retaining his anonymity? A guy who had patently
never thought about her again since then? Of course he
wasn't pleased, and he would never be pleased. Of course
he was still hoping that there was some mistake or that she
was a lying schemer.

After all, Alexandros Christakis had no feelings for her.
She had been a casual sexual amusement when he'd been
bored and at a loose end. Turning up again now as she had,
looking scruffy and down on her luck, she was nothing but
a source of embarrassment to a male of his sophistication

and wealth. Add in her announcement about the twins, and she became the stuff of most single guys' nightmares, she reflected painfully. He didn't love her and he didn't want to be with her, so what could fatherhood mean to him? Men only wanted a family with women they cared about. Alexandros wouldn't want her children. Well, that was all right, she told herself doggedly. All she wanted and needed from him was financial help.

The limo came to a halt. In an abrupt movement that revealed his stress level, Alexandros broke free of his shield of reserve and closed a lean brown hand over hers. 'If they are my children, I swear that I will support you in every way possible,' he breathed in a driven undertone. 'Give me your mobile number.'

'I don't have a phone.'

He dug a card out of his pocket, printed a number on it and extended it to her. 'It's my personal number.'

His *personal* number. Her eyes prickled and stung like mad. She wanted to scrunch the card up and throw it at him, because he had been so careful not to give her that number eighteen months earlier. Her throat was so thick with tears that she could hardly breathe, much less hurl the tart comment she wanted to fling. She had loved him so much. It had been a savage hurt when he'd rejected her, and to be forced back into his radius and made to feel as undesirable as the plague was salt in that wound.

Alexandros watched her cross the busy pavement. She moved with the sinuous grace and light step of a dancer. He tore his attention from her, refusing to acknowledge that reflection, and the door closed, leaving him alone with his bleak thoughts. If a man could be said to have ditched a woman with good intentions, he was that man. Now it seemed that although he owned the race in the cut-throat world of high finance, his private life was destined to be a disaster area. Once again he had screwed up. Once again he would have to pay the price. As she had paid it. Just what he needed, he reflected with a bitterness he could not suppress: a guilt trip that would last the rest of his life.

How likely was it that her children were his? He remembered Katie's indiscreet, straight-from-the heart forthrightness. He had found her honesty such a novelty. There had been no half-truths and no evasions. Very refreshing—until she'd said those fatal words he could not stand to hear on another woman's lips. *I love you*—that little phrase that Ianthe had made so much her own.

Why had he let Katie get out of the limo? Chances were she was telling the truth and he *was* the father of her twins. He suppressed a shudder. He knew exactly what was required of him. He knew he had absolutely no business thinking about himself or about how he felt. He had dug his own grave. He recalled that Katie didn't even have a phone. He swore long and low under his breath. Perhaps she needed food more.

'You have appointments, boss,' Cyrus remarked in an apologetic tone.

Alexandros ignored that reminder. Acting purely on impulse, he went to Harrods and bought an enormous hamper, and the latest mobile phone in Katie's favourite colour. His own out-of-character behaviour seriously spooked him. He called his lawyer. His lawyer called for legal reinforcements and urged crisis talks, DNA specialists and extreme prudence. Alexandros might still have acted on his gut instincts, had it not been for the timely reminder of the potential for a huge scandal. Personal visits and gifts, it was pointed out, would only reinforce any claims made against him, and add to the risk of sordid publicity.

'Your grandparents…'

The reminder was sufficient to halt Alexandros in his tracks. Pelias and Calliope Christakis would be very distressed if an unsavoury scandal engulfed their grandson. The older couple were not of an age where their continuing good health could be taken for granted either. In the short term, Alexandros grudgingly accepted that a discreet and cautious course would be wisest.

Katie was intercepted before she could climb the stairs to her room.

'Miss Fletcher?'

It was the same thin fair man she had seen watching her in the foyer of CTK bank. 'Yes?'

He handed her his card as an introduction. 'I'm Trev. I work for the *Daily Globe*. Mind me asking what your connection to Alexandros Christakis is?'

Taken aback, Katie muttered, 'I don't know what you're talking about—'

'But you do. You just got out of the bloke's limo!'

'You saw me? Did you follow me all the way from the bank? And to my friend's as well?' Katie was unnerved by that awareness, and turned towards the stairs again.

The reporter was in her way. 'I hear you have a couple of kids…'

'What's that got to do with you?'

'Christakis is a very interesting guy. If you have anything to tell us about him it could be well worth your while,' he told her with a meaningful look. 'People don't talk about him. He lives in a world most of us can only envy. So anything of an exciting personal nature would have a very high cash value.'

Katie hesitated, distaste filling her. She wanted to tell

him to get lost and leave her alone. If only Alexandros had given her a more concrete promise of support than a phone number! Leanne had said that she should be prepared to do anything to give Toby and Connor a better start in life. But talking to a newspaper in return for money struck her as sleazy, and she wanted to think that she was above doing that sort of thing. And yet she was also painfully aware that it was her job to provide her children with a decent home, and achieving that would require cold hard cash.

'We're on your trail now, so if there's any dirt to dig we'll find it anyway.' Threat and warning were linked in Trev's hopeful appraisal. 'So why don't you make it easier for us and turn a profit too?'

'I'm not interested.' Even as she spoke, Katie did not know whether or not she was making the right decision.

An hour later she went back to Leanne's, to pick up Toby and Connor. While her friend saw her mother out of the flat, Katie scooped up her sons, one at a time out of the buggy, and hugged them tight. After a busy morning of occupation, Toby gave her a huge sunny smile, and Connor laughed.

'So, *tell*…' Leanne urged impatiently. 'What happened? Did you get to see Alexandros?'

Katie explained, while her friend listened with avid interest and made her describe the limo in detail.

'Alexandros is obviously stinking rich.' A calculating expression formed on Leanne's pretty face. 'And the best offer he can make you is a DNA test?' she sneered. 'He'll need to do a lot better than that!'

'He was shocked… I'll give him a couple of days and see what happens.' Katie displayed the card she had been given by the journalist to the brunette.

'Whoopy-do!' Leanne snatched the card to study it, more impressed by the interest of the *Daily Globe* than by anything else. 'This Trev took the trouble to follow you? Hey, Alexandros must be a real celebrity! And you turned the reporter's offer *down*? Are you out of your tiny mind?'

'I have to give Alexandros a chance to help us first.'

'But if the press find out whose kids Toby and Connor are without your input, you won't make any money at all!'

Katie was beginning to feel uncomfortable. 'I know, but I don't think anyone will work out what my relationship was with Alexandros any time soon. I mean, nobody knows about us—'

'You could make pots of money out of this, Katie. Haven't you got the guts to go for it?' her friend demanded

'Alexandros would hate that kind of publicity, and he'd never forgive me for it.'

'So what? What's he to you?'

'He'll always be the twins' father. I don't want to make an enemy of him. Flogging our story to the newspapers has to be a last resort for me.'

Leanne gave her a scornful look. 'You're being really stupid about this. There's money to be made. Your problem is that you've still got feelings for that bastard—'

Katie was affronted by that suggestion. 'No, I haven't!'

'Much good it'll do you. He doesn't want to know now, does he?' Leanne sniped, and soon after that Katie thought it wisest to thank the brunette for looking after the twins and go.

Mid-morning the following day, a young man in casual clothing came to her door. 'Are you Katie Fletcher?'

At her nod of confirmation, he extended a mobile phone to her.

'I'm a solicitor, engaged to represent a certain person's interests, Miss Fletcher,' the brisk voice on the phone informed her. 'I'm sure you'll understand the need for discretion in this case. Are you willing to undergo DNA testing?'

Katie was taken by surprise, but recognised that such speed of action was essentially an Alexandros Christakis trait. 'Yes…'

'Then sign the consent form and the matter will be taken care of immediately, with the minimum of disruption.'

An envelope and a pen were passed to her, the phone returned. Her caller departed. She drew out a brief document, scanned it with strained eyes and then scrawled her signature. Alexandros was doing what came naturally to him. It was insulting and humiliating, but also a necessary evil if she was to prove her claim. Within half an hour a doctor arrived with a medical bag. He explained that the test consisted of painless mouth swabs being taken from her and the twins. In a matter of minutes he had carried out the procedure and smoothly taken his leave again.

She walked the floor that evening, trying to soothe Toby. Although it was barely nine o'clock, someone banged on the wall to complain, and a man knocked at the door and asked her to keep her kids quiet because he was a shift worker trying to get some sleep. Tears were tracking down Katie's weary face while she struggled to quieten Toby, who seemed to have no more notion of sleeping at night than an owl. It was impossible for her not to look back and wonder how her life had drifted so far off the course she had assumed it would follow…

After Katie's English father had died, her mother had taken her daughter back to Ireland to live. Katie had enjoyed a happy childhood in a small town where everyone had known everyone else. Armed with an honours degree in Economics, she had been ecstatic when she'd got her first job as a PA in London. But when her mother had fallen ill she had had to resign and return home.

In spite of her ill health, Maura Fletcher had insisted on keeping up a couple of part-time jobs. Fearful of losing her livelihood, the older woman had only been persuaded to take the doctor's advice and rest when Katie had agreed to stand in for her until she regained her strength.

Maura had acted as caretaker and occasional house-keeper at a superb contemporary house which overlooked a sea inlet a few miles from their home. Owned by a German industrialist and rarely occupied, the property lay down a long gated track and enjoyed an incredibly private and beautiful setting. Katie had one day prepared the house for the occupation of a single mystery guest. A car accident had put the two domestic staff travelling with Alexandros out of commission and the rental agency, unaware that Katie was doing her mother's job for her, had recommended her parent as temporary cook and cleaner.

A fax had followed, detailing more exact requirements, and Katie had been staggered by the number of rules she was expected to observe, ranging from meals to be served at rigid hours and a duty on her part to being both invisible and silent. On the other hand, the salary offered had been generous enough to bring a delighted smile to her mother's anxious face, and the cutting-edge equipment being installed in the office with a sea view and a balcony had suggested that the guest would be much too busy to pay heed to the amateur level of the household help. Of course, accustomed as Alexandros was to perfection in every field, he had refused to settle for less, and Katie, secretly resenting the role of servant, had refused to be suitably humble. That they should clash had been inevitable.

No passage of time could eradicate Katie's memory of

her first glimpse of Alexandros. After he had arrived by helicopter, he had gone straight down to the seashore. From about twenty yards away she had watched him, dumbstruck by his sleek, dark, masculine magnificence. Clad in jeans and a husky grey cashmere sweater, and even with his black hair tousled by the breeze and designer stubble obscuring his stubborn jawline, he had bewitched her. She had never known a man could be that physically beautiful, or seem so alone and isolated. Wanton desire and longing had leapt up in her that very first moment, and she had never been able to overcome it…

Someone rapped at the door and she studied it in dismay, fearing another complaint just when Toby had mercifully subsided to the occasional long-drawn-out whimper of dissatisfaction. Tiptoeing over, she eased the door open a crack, for she was dressed in her pyjamas, and then fell back in complete confusion.

'May I come in?' Alexandros asked grimly, his dignity having been severely ruffled by Cyrus's insistence that it was necessary for his employer to enter the building in a clandestine manner and via an alley full of dustbins. An instant later Alexandros' irritation had vanished into the ether—a triviality when set next to the cold shock of his surroundings…

CHAPTER THREE

ALEXANDROS was a man of action, and playing a waiting game when Katie had asked for help ran contrary to his masculine code of ethics. Ignoring legal advice and doing what *he* felt had to be done came much more naturally to his dominant nature.

But Alexandros had never before come into personal contact with the kind of poverty that now confronted him. The room was tiny, cramped and shabby. A clothes airer stacked with damp washing, a pram and a bed were crammed up against a cot from which he swiftly averted his attention. In the single patch of space between the battered wardrobe and a sink stacked with baby bottles stood Katie. His golden gaze arrowed in on her like a laser. Against the riot of copper curls tumbling round her startled face her eyes shimmered green as emeralds, and, that fast, his body responded with a testosterone-charged surge of sexual hunger.

Even as the unreasoning shock of that lust hit, the darker side of him revelled in its resurgence. Instantly memories he had buried so deep he only dreamt about them surfaced. Katie up against the kitchen wall, tumbled in a pile of white linen, in a bubble bath with a ring of candles round her. The candles had been snuffed out by the overflowing water when he had hauled her up into his arms. Time after time he had discovered that he could never get enough of her, and that lack of control so foreign to his temperament had gone very much against the grain.

'I wasn't expecting you…' Katie could feel the tension in the air leaping and crackling round her like mini-lightning bolts, and she could not dredge her attention from him. He had always had that effect on her. He walked into room and owned it and the occupants until he chose to release them from the power of his potent presence and forceful personality.

'If I hadn't had a dinner engagement I would have called earlier.' Belatedly registering the brief camisole and shorts she wore, Alexandros was striving not to notice the milky pale swell of her round breasts above and below the worn fabric. His even white teeth gritted while he tried to work out why she should have such a dramatic effect on his libido.

'I'm glad you're here,' Katie admitted, feeling that her faith in him had been justified. She was pleased and proud that he had not lived down to Leanne's low expectations.

A little snuffling whimper drifted from the cot. Alexandros went rigid. A tiny hand curled round a bar in the cot and a small face appeared behind the bars. Gripped by the most excruciating curiosity, in spite of his resistance to the very idea of parenthood, Alexandros slowly moved closer. Katie's acquiescence to the demand for DNA testing without a single objection had convinced him that she was very probably telling him the truth.

'Boys?' Alexandros almost whispered, looking down at the two curly dark heads.

'Yes.'

'But not identical.' The cynosure of two pairs of curious

dark brown eyes, Alexandros was frozen to the spot. They were his. One observant glance was sufficient to persuade him of that reality. For both small faces bore compelling evidence of their Christakis lineage: straight brows that were a light baby version of his own, an early hint of the family cleft chin that even his grandfather carried, skin and eyes a little paler than his, but hair as blue-black. The curls were their mother's, and the only proof that he could see of her input into their gene pool. His level regard was being returned by the babies without fear. He was a father, he registered in shock, whether he liked it or not.

'No,' she agreed in a taut rush, for she was desperate to know what he was thinking. 'But well-spotted! At first glance most people do think the twins are identical.'

Unaffected by that hint of a compliment, Alexandros continued to survey the two little boys with brooding force. There they were, sharing the same cot, like orphans in some squalid children's home. His sons, his responsibility. Life as he knew it was over, he conceded bleakly. His freedom had just been imprisoned and was awaiting sentence to be hung drawn and quartered. There would be no escape from the agonies ahead. He would have to offer her marriage. It was his own fault. He had brought this punishment on himself. What a mess. What a bloody mess!

One of the babies cried, and she bent over the side of the cot to lift the child, treating Alexandros to a provocative view of her apple-shaped derriere. Tiny and slight she might be, but she was still one hundred per cent woman in the places that mattered, he found himself thinking—until he cracked down on that inappropriate reflection.

'I think you should get some clothes on,' Alexandros told her, with the censorious air of a Puritan being tempted by a loose woman.

Only then registering that she was hardly dressed for
visitors, Katie straightened, clutching Connor, her face
pink with embarrassment. 'For goodness' sake, I'm
wearing my pyjamas.'

'It's barely nine-thirty in the evening—'

'So? I sleep whenever I get the chance!' She stuffed her
son into Alexandros's arms without even thinking about
what she was doing, and turned away in a hurry to snatch
up her dressing gown. Her cheeks were burning. Had he
told her to cover up because he believed she was trying to
tempt him with her body? Did she look that desperate?
Perhaps she did, she thought painfully.

As Katie thrust Connor into his arms, Alexandros turned
to stone. Connor also froze. The little boy then reacted to
his father's extreme tension by opening his mouth and
howling like a burglar alarm. Aghast, Alexandros studied
the screaming child and put him straight down on the
carpet. 'No more,' he told his son in reproving Greek, as
if he was a misbehaving seven-year-old.

As Connor's ear-splitting cry mounted to a shriek, Katie
scooped him up and hugged his squirming little body pro-
tectively close. 'How could you just put him down like
that? Don't you think he has feelings?'

Alexandros winced as Toby loosed a first warning
squeal from the cot. 'I'm a stranger to him. I thought I had
frightened him. I have never held a child before.'

'Neither had I when the twins were born. But I had no
choice but to learn!'

'I don't need to learn,' Alexandros drawled, sardonic in
tone and equally dry. 'I can afford a nanny.'

'I'm thrilled for you.'

Backing off to the door, Alexandros watched her efforts
to placate the babies. With two little screeching horrors to

look after, it was little wonder that she looked exhausted.
He held at bay the knowledge that he had helped to create
those screeching horrors now dogging her daily existence,
and imposed a strict mental block on the noise of their cries
while he watched Katie. He was still fiercely determined
to penetrate the mystery of her attraction, since she bore
not the smallest resemblance to the women he normally
went for. She wasn't tall, she wasn't blonde, and she wasn't
ravishingly beautiful.

Tiny and slender though she was, however, there was
something about the arrangement of her delicate features
and the unexpectedly lush curve of breast and hip that
raised her to a seriously appetising level of desirability,
Alexandros acknowledged abstractedly. He considered the
reality that she had conceived and given birth to his
children. All of a sudden that seemed an extraordinarily
sexy achievement to him. He imagined sliding his hands
under the thin camisole she wore, and the exquisite feel of
the silky skin on her narrow ribcage beneath his palms
before he curved his fingers up and round...

'Just what is the matter with you?' Katie launched at
Alexandros in almost sobbing frustration. She could not
cope when both the twins cried at once, and was enraged by
his supreme detachment from the rising decibel level in the
room. 'Haven't you got any interest in your own children?'

Unwillingly forced from the realms of erotic fantasy,
Alexandros dealt her an enquiring glance from below his
luxuriant black lashes, the faintest hint of colour scoring
his stunning high cheekbones. 'I'm here,' he fielded without expression. 'That should tell you something.'

'That you don't *want* to be here!' Katie condemned
helplessly, devastated by his failure even to ask the twins'
names. 'That's what your attitude is telling me!'

'How may I help?' Alexandros ground out, his accent very thick.

'Lift Toby…'

Alexandros approached the cot, squared his shoulders, reached in and closed his hands round the wriggling baby. He performed that feat with the same enthusiasm with which he might have stuck his hands in a blazing fire. *Toby.* Alexandros sounded the name under his breath, reading the look of anxious surprise in the child's brown eyes as he lifted him. He drew Toby awkwardly closer. More able to rate the experience the second time around, he was amazed at how light in weight Toby was—and then transfixed by the big smile that transformed the little boy's face. That open happy grin reminded Alexandros very much of Pelias, and made Toby feel familiar.

Engaged in soothing Connor, it was a moment or two before Katie registered that peace had fallen again. She glanced up and saw Alexandros smiling at her eldest son. That smile stopped her heart in its tracks, made her chest go all tight, rousing memories so painful that hot tears burned the back of her eyes. Once, and for a very brief period, Alexandros had looked at her like that, and she had wanted to turn somersaults and sing with the sheer joy of living. It had not occurred to her then that losing him would hurt like hell, that the world he had made seem so bright and full of promise could just as swiftly turn grey and threatening. But now, she reminded herself doggedly, she was no longer so naive and trusting. Expecting more from Alexandros Christakis than help with the rent would be asking for trouble.

'What is his brother called?' Alexandros enquired.

'Connor.'

'We will have to discuss the requirements of this situation.' Alexandros utilised the business terminology that he was most at ease with.

'I'm not looking for much from you. I only want us to have somewhere decent to live,' Katie muttered with low-pitched urgency, as she settled Connor carefully back into the cot and held her arms out for his brother.

Alexandros surrendered Toby. He straightened his broad shoulders, his wide, sensual mouth compressing. Could she really be so clueless? Or was he supposed to be impressed by her pretence of innocence? She could hardly be ignorant of the fact that the simple act of having had his children would turn out to be a highly profitable enterprise.

'I'll move you out of here as soon as possible,' Alexandros responded. 'Tomorrow, I should think.'

Katie spun back to study him in wide-eyed astonishment. 'Tomorrow? Are you serious?'

'I would take you home with me now…' Dark golden eyes rested on her for a heartbeat, with an intensity that made her mouth run dry and the skin at the nape of her neck prickle. 'But it would be too unsettling to move the children at this hour.'

An uneasy laugh fell from her lips, for she assumed that that reference to taking her home was a joke—and not one in the best of taste. 'Luckily for you, I'm not expecting to go home with you. I'll be more than happy to be placed in a position to afford a small flat for the three of us.' Her colour heightened, she avoided his gaze and jerked a narrow shoulder in an awkward gesture. 'My goodness, why is anything involving money so embarrassing to talk about?'

Alexandros, who had never found money a source of embarrassment, and could not imagine ever doing so, was unmoved. 'Naturally I have no intention of leaving you to raise the twins alone.'

Katie tied the sash on her dressing gown with nervous hands and said nothing. So he was planning to take on some sort of paternal role? A visit once a month? Sandwiched in between business trips and dirty weekends with gorgeous women?

'I'm not a total bastard,' Alexandros breathed.

With care, Katie averted her gaze from his. She deemed it wisest not to comment, for she had, after all, spent eighteen months thinking of him in exactly those terms. He had taken her virginity, got her pregnant, dumped her and left her with a dud phone number for emergencies. In addition, the one website she had lingered on after she'd found out about his connection to CTK Bank had described him as a notoriously successful womaniser with a taste for supermodels. In comparison she was nothing and nobody, and she was determined not to let herself forget that demeaning truth. This time around she intended to keep her silly feet on the ground in his radius.

Alexandros, who was as much a stranger to criticism as to female disapproval, was annoyed by her unresponsive silence. 'Katie…I have honour.'

She lifted her head, collided with the scorching gold challenge of his potent gaze, and felt the burn of his anger. It had the most disturbing effect on her, for she could not help recalling that he could go from anger to passion in the space of a moment. That icy façade concealed a molten core. Her mind a hopeless blank, she snatched in a stark lungful of air, suddenly maddeningly aware of the little knot of awareness forming in the pit of her stomach. Her breasts felt heavy, the tender peaks pinching taut below her clothing. Heat was pulsing through her. She let her head angle back and slightly to one side, copper curls trailing, lashes lowering over softened green eyes.

'Alexandros…' she framed shakily, in the grip of something that had very swiftly got stronger than she was.

As alert to her every signal as a natural-born predator, Alexandros had switched to the same channel of communication without even being aware of it. He was studying the moist pink softness of her generous mouth with strictly dishonourable intentions. If he kissed her, she would stop talking at him, voicing stupid sentiments that could only offend. He was already so hot for her he ached, and he was savouring that fast, fierce arousal, acknowledging how long it had been since he had wanted any woman to such a degree. He closed a hand over her shoulder and tugged her to him, curving strong hands below her hips to lift her up to him.

Katie shut her eyes tight shut at the first intoxicating taste of him, let her head fall back in invitation, her lips open. He took advantage of her offer with the devastating sensuality that had always been her downfall. He did not ask, he demanded, and that raw, unapologetically masculine urgency turned her bones to water below her skin. It was like hitching a ride on a rocket. Her head was in a whirl. She could hardly breathe as her body reacted to the overwhelming surge of excitement with excruciating enthusiasm. On all systems go, she quivered and clung to his broad shoulders, moaning beneath the erotic plunge of his tongue.

It was an unfamiliar sound that stopped Alexandros in the very act of bringing her down on the bed behind her. Stepping back from her with a hoarse exclamation, he focussed on the baby watching them with pronounced interest through the cot bars. He was appalled that he had let control slip that far. He had forgotten about the children. His mind could not encompass how he could possibly have forgotten the presence of the twins he had only just learned were his.

'I shouldn't have done that. It was inappropriate,' he breathed icily.

Katie reeled back from him on weak legs. She was seeing mental stars, and sweet sensation was still shimmying in seductive waves through her newly awakened body. She knew she ought to hate herself for succumbing to that passionate kiss, but in reality she just wanted Alexandros to flatten her to the bed and have his wicked way with her. Shame infiltrated at that mortifying awareness, but even so there was just one question that she needed to ask.

'Is there someone else…?' She had to know. Indeed, she tried and failed to stifle that overpowering need to know.

The silence lay there like a giant chasm, yawning suddenly below her feet. She could feel herself falling from a terrifying height and drowning in that horrendous silence. She always said the wrong thing with him. Like *I love you*—and he had left the country, never mind her, behind. Her fingernails scored crescents that hurt into her palms. She wanted to wring her own throat, tie a knot in her tongue, for she didn't have to look at him to work out the answer. The atmospheric vibes were full of warning flares. He was such a player, such a diplomat. She could feel him wincing at her lack of cool. This was a guy who could barely cross a room without getting a female come-on…

'This is not the moment to get into that.' Alexandros was sincerely appalled by such reckless in-your-face candour. He surveyed her downbent copper head. She looked so vulnerable. Why did she always make him feel such a bastard?

'You shouldn't have touched me—'

'You wanted to be touched.' He tossed a slim package down on the bed. 'This is for you. I'll be in touch tomorrow.'

It was the latest phone—very thin, very small, and in

her favourite colour. The door shut fast on his exit. Dazed, she blinked. Maybe he was scared she still fancied herself in love with him. She swallowed the great fat lump in her throat. He was gone. The room felt emptier than empty, sucked bare of life. She wanted to throw herself up against the door and sob like a baby. She didn't like him, and she knew he was bad for her. But that didn't mean that she had learned how to stop loving him, or craving what was bad for her…

Alexandros got back in the limo and received a call from a close friend—the titled owner of a well-known tabloid newspaper. 'I thought I should warn you that there's a rumour the *Globe* may run with a big story on you this week…very hush-hush stuff.'

Alexandros tensed. The paparazzi were always on his trail. They could not get enough photos of him, the women he entertained, the lifestyle he enjoyed. He refused to credit that word about Katie and the twins could already have leaked into the public domain. But he contacted his press officer to check whether or not he had been asked for comment. There had been no such approach. An uneasy feeling persisted when he recalled Katie angrily telling him after he'd spoken to her on the phone at the bank that he would not be able to say that she hadn't given him a chance.

He called her on the mobile he had given her.

It took Katie a second or two to identify the source of the ringing, and she snatched the phone up, fearful that the twins would be disturbed. 'Er…hello?'

'Have you talked to any journalists about us?' Alexandros enquired, in the most casual of tones.

Katie reddened with instantaneous guilt. 'No…'

'Are you certain?' Alexandros murmured, with a lethal cool that trickled down her spine like an executioner's warning. 'If I was to find out that you had lied about this, I would be seriously ticked-off.'

'I'm not lying…but I *was* approached by a reporter,' she confided, and hastily furnished the details of that encounter.

'But you told him nothing?' Alexandros checked.

'Absolutely nothing,' she confirmed.

'I don't tolerate press intrusion into my life.'

'I don't know why you're telling me this—'

'You're now a part of that life, and I would be very displeased if any revelations of even the most innocent kind involving either myself or the children were to appear in print. As far as the Christakis family is concerned, *all* publicity is bad publicity.'

'Right—I'll consider myself duly warned…okay?' But, feisty though that response was, Katie was secretly cherishing the assurance that he already considered her a part of his life.

'Okay.' Alexandros ended the call.

His grandparents would have to be carefully prepared for what he had to tell them about Katie and the twins. He was not in a hurry to tackle that challenge, so he would await the official DNA results. He would have to fly out to Greece to break the news personally, and in as gentle a manner as possible. But, even so, the old couple would be distressed. His lean, strong face clenched hard. He sincerely hoped there would be no reference to old history, no reminder of his own less then satisfactory start in life. He had every intention of doing what he knew to be his duty. Hadn't he done so all his life to date? Since when had he put his own needs first?

Alexandros was wakened soon after dawn by an urgent call from Pelias Christakis.

'Is it true? Is it true that you are the father of a pair of baby boys?' his grandfather demanded in a quavering voice of disbelief. 'Or is it a shocking calumny?'

Alexandros thrust back the duvet and vaulted out of bed, stark naked.

'I have friends in the publishing world,' Pelias shared. 'But if this startling story is genuine, I would have preferred to have heard it from your lips.'

While volcanic fury was taking hold of Alexandros, Katie was suffering an equally rude awakening to events. Someone was hammering on the door, and when she opened it a man stuck a microphone in her face.

'Katie? Would you like to comment on today's spread in the *Daily Globe*? Is Alexandros Christakis the father of your kids?'

'What spread?' she gasped.

With a cheerful grin, she was passed a newspaper. Thrusting the door shut, she bolted it and unfolded the paper.

Billionaire's Secret Babies of Shame ran the headline on the front page. Below was a photo of Alexandros giving a speech under a world trade banner, juxtaposed with a photo of a drab jean-clad young girl wheeling a buggy. Her mouth fell inelegantly wide when she realised that the girl was herself, and that the picture had been taken on the street outside without her knowledge.

Someone was banging on the door again and shouting her name, and the mobile phone beside the bed was ringing. Her tummy in apprehensive knots, Katie ignored those demands for her attention to tear open the paper and find the rest of the story. *The Banker and the Maid* shouted the sub-heading. She shuddered. She had *not* been the maid! But hadn't Alexandros once awarded her that lowly label? In disbelief she saw a recent picture of herself and her children in a local park, with Toby and Connor's faces carefully obscured. Leanne had taken that picture. How had the *Globe* got hold of that? And the one precious stolen photo she had of Alexandros? There he was, working at a laptop, black hair flopping over his brow, lashes so long they were silhouetted against the light along with his classic profile. That had been kept in a box she had left to be stored at Leanne's apartment. Had she been burgled?

Her mind shied away from the possibility that her closest friend could have betrayed her.

Stretching out a reluctant hand, Katie answered the phone. 'Please don't blame me for this….'

Alexandros was much too clever to risk frightening her into flight. 'I believe your accommodation is under siege by the press?'

'There's even people at my door,' she confided nervously.

'Don't worry about packing anything, and don't open that door to speak to anyone. My security team will get you and the children out of there within the hour. When my security chief is ready, you'll be alerted on this number.'

It had now gone silent in the corridor outside. She surmised that her neighbours had complained about the noise and the hotel manager had made her unwanted callers leave the premises. She washed and dressed in a frantic panic, and did the same for Toby and Connor. Having given them a drink and some baby rice, she filled a bag. Alexandros could not be expected to understand how impossible it was to go anywhere with young children without certain necessities. That done, she made herself lift the *Daily Globe* again, and read the inside story.

In actuality she only read the first line and got no further.

Alexandros Christakis, who married shipping heiress Ianthe Kalakos at the age of twenty, may have a secret family…

Married? He was married? Alexandros was a married man? He had a wife? He had had a wife when he'd slept with her? When he'd got her pregnant with the twins? Devastated by that new knowledge, Katie collapsed down on the bed. She pushed the newspaper away from her in anguish and disgust. Tears lashed her eyes. What a total clown she was! So besotted that she had refused to face what should have been obvious eighteen months ago! No wonder Alexandros had such a thing about publicity and discretion. No wonder he hadn't given her a proper phone number! When she had told Leanne about Alexandros, the brunette's very first question had been, 'Is he married?' She had fallen in love with another woman's husband.

Now he was offering to come to her rescue, no doubt determined to swiftly spirit her away from any contact with the press. Ought she to allow him to do that? She drew in a quivering breath. Even if he *was* married, she still needed his help to give the boys a decent upbringing, and the twins were entitled to that support. But what a louse she had picked to get involved with!

Her phone rang again. She lifted it. A man who introduced himself as Cyrus announced that he was waiting in the corridor to escort her out of the building. She recognised the big thickset chauffeur from her first trip in Alexandros's limo. He shook his head at the buggy and lifted Toby out of his seat. She hooked her baby bag on her shoulder and grabbed Connor. In silence they descended the back stairs and left by the fire exit. A limo was waiting at the end of the alley.

Alexandros had a wife. That awful awareness slunk up on Katie afresh, and she bit the soft underside of her lower lip hard in punishment. Desperate to give her thoughts another direction, she dug out her mobile phone and punched in Leanne's number. Her friend answered almost immediately.

'It's Katie—'

The brunette burst straight into speech. 'What do you want me to say? The money was there for the asking and I went for it. I've got debts…all right? I needed the cash. I'm sorry, but survival of the fittest and all that…'

'You went through my personal belongings to get those photos. They were private and they were mine—'

'Your personal belongings are cluttering up *my* bedroom! Maybe Christakis will pay his dues for the twins now. Maybe you'll find out that I've done you a favour!'

'I'll pick up my stuff as soon as I can.' Hurt, because she had been very fond of Leanne, Katie finished the call. She had trusted the other girl one hundred per cent. But how close had their friendship really been? She had not known that Leanne was in debt. Survival of the fittest?

A married man. Alexandros belonged to another woman, who was probably gutted by the tale that that newspaper had printed. Katie's conscience went into convulsions. A further apprehension assailed her. What if that sordid story somehow stretched as far as New Zealand, where her mother now lived in happy ignorance of the fact that she was the grandmother of two illegitimate kids? Katie paled at that prospect. Maura would be distraught at the secret that her daughter had kept from her. As the ramifications of the *Daily Globe*'s revelations began to sink in, angry bitterness began to gain the edge over the guilt Katie felt at Leanne's role in her plight.

Toby and Connor were sound asleep in their car seats when the limousine finally pulled up outside a vast country house. Katie climbed out very slowly, for she had not been prepared for such an imposing destination.

'There are staff here at Dove Hall to take care of the little boys,' Cyrus told her when she hovered, her green eyes huge as she studied the great sandstone historic pile in front of her. 'Mr Christakis is waiting to see you.'

Rosy colour warmed Katie's triangular face. She straightened her slender back and lifted her chin. 'Good…'

A housekeeper was waiting in the wide elegant hall, and Katie was shown straight into a pale blue drawing room with a spectacular painted ceiling. The grandeur of her surroundings made her feel more nervous than ever.

A door at the other end of the big room swung back on its hinges beneath an impatient hand. Katie spun round. Alexandros was framed in the ornate doorway. He looked exceptionally tall and austere, and his darkly handsome features were set like granite in a blizzard.

'So…' Green eyes raw with angry pain, Katie was determined to get what she had to say in first. 'Exactly when were you planning to tell me that you have a wife?'

CHAPTER FOUR

'As a red herring, that won't cut it,' Alexandros told her forbiddingly.

'Evading the question won't win you any points with me either,' Katie fielded, squaring up to him, equally set on confrontation. 'You know very well that you didn't tell me that you were married, and that's inexcusable—'

'I'm not married,' Alexandros cut in.

'You're divorced?' Involuntarily Katie hesitated as she made that deduction. Some of her anger dissipated, curiosity sparking, so that it was an effort to fire the next phase of attack. 'But you must still have been married when you came over to Ireland!'

'No.'

Katie waited for him to add some form of explanation, but that one bald word seemed to be all that was coming her way. 'I don't think I can believe you…'

Alexandros shrugged a broad shoulder.

'I have a right to know—'

'You don't have a right to know *anything* about my marriage,' Alexandros delivered, regarding her with a punishing degree of disdain.

Katie went very pale.

'You don't have good reason to doubt my word either.'

Katie found her voice again. 'Oh, yes, I do!'

Alexandros shifted a lean brown hand in a silencing motion. 'I have no time for this. If you did not have those little boys, you would not be here in this house now.'

'Did you imagine I might think otherwise?' Katie was rigid with tension. 'You didn't exactly overwhelm me with a welcome at the bank, did you?'

'You know what I'm saying to you. Last night you listened to my warning and you swore that you hadn't talked to the press. I find it hard to credit that you had the nerve, but you *lied* to me—'

'I didn't!'

'Keep quiet,' Alexandros countered with icy emphasis. 'I didn't trust you fully last night, but I was willing to give you the benefit of the doubt. I will not make that mistake again. How could you be so stupid as to alienate me when you're dependent on me?'

Off-balanced by that attack, and with her pride smarting beyond belief, Katie sucked in a stark breath. 'I am not and I never will be dependent on you! I'm a lot more independent than that—'

'Is that how you describe selling tacky stories about me to a tabloid? Independence?' Alexandros derided.

Her heart-shaped face flamed and her hands balled into fists.

'Don't you dare even think about throwing something at me,' Alexandros told her softly.

Angry embarrassment consumed Katie, for she considered that taunt to be a very low blow. 'I wasn't going to.'

A level ebony brow climbed. 'No? I was under the impression that you always throw things when you're losing an argument.'

'You're not arguing with me, you're sneering at me, and I can rise above it—'

'You'll need a hell of a long ladder to rise above the vulgarity of your current status,' he slotted in with offensive cool.

Katie lifted a hand in a furious motion. 'Of course it doesn't occur to you that I might not have been the one to sell that story to the *Globe*!'

Alexandros vented a sardonic laugh. 'Hey…is that a unicorn outside the window?'

'Right now, you're just reminding me of all the things I really hate about you!' Katie launched.

Alexandros dealt her a look of burning contempt, and rage rose inside her with explosive ease. His bone-deep arrogance, his inbred conviction of his superiority, and that quality of insolence he exuded literally made her feel lightheaded with temper. But she struggled to control her annoyance, because she knew how much he cherished his privacy and it *had* been violated by the *Globe*. Furthermore, she might not have been the one to profit, but she did feel responsible for what her friend had done.

'When I spoke to you last night I was telling the truth when I said I hadn't talked to that newspaper guy. I can understand that you are angry—'

'Why would I be angry?' Alexandros drawled silkily.

'And I'm sorry about what's happened—'

'Sorry is a waste of your breath. It will be a very long time before I forget this episode.'

'It wasn't me who sold that story…it was my friend, Leanne,' Katie told him heavily.

'There's a *herd* of unicorns out on the lawn,' Alexandros murmured with biting clarity. 'Why are you feeding me this nonsense?'

Katie gritted her teeth together. 'I will say it just one more time. It wasn't *me*.'

'You took photos of me in Ireland without my knowledge,' Alexandros condemned. 'Their appearance today in the *Globe* confirms your guilt.'

'Cameraphone…stupid.' Her nose wrinkled, her throat muscles tightening as she thought of how desperately she had once wanted a picture of him.

'Stolen photos—'

'Oh, shut up!' Rage and pain coalesced and mushroomed up inside Katie like a pressure cooker, venting steam without warning. 'You're the most incredible control freak! So I was infatuated with you, and I went sneaking around like a silly kid, so that I could snatch some idiotic photos of you with my phone…get over it!'

A faint hint of colour now scored his fabulous cheekbones. 'And those photos appeared in that filthy article—'

'Aren't you lucky that I didn't take any revealing ones? Your problem is that you don't know what a *real* problem is, so you make a fuss over trivial things—'

'Trivial?' Alexandros dealt her a searing look of charged disbelief. 'According to that tabloid rag, I pour vintage champagne over my women and then I shag them in hot tubs…that's when I'm not making them dress up as French maids for a dirty thrill!'

'You're joking…' For a moment, Katie studied him aghast, because she had not read the article in the *Globe* beyond that enervating first line relating to his marital status. But her horror was entirely on her own behalf as she imagined rumours of such shocking shenanigans reaching her mother and her stepfather in New Zealand. 'What are you complaining about?' she asked fiercely. 'So all the guys think you're a heck of a lad? But I get labelled as a slut who plays sex games for your benefit! That is just so typical of the world we live in—'

Totally disconcerted though he was by her attitude, Alexandros gave not an inch, and breathed with icy restraint. 'Whose fault is that? You concocted the grossest lies to sell that tripe.'

Katie felt something snap inside her. Her angry despair at his refusal to believe her claims rose to such a choking peak of emotion that she couldn't trust herself to speak. Instead she shifted her hands in a clumsy gesture of dismissal.

'Katie…'

Ignoring him, Katie turned on her heel to walk towards the door.

'What are you doing?'

'I'm leaving.'

'Where do you think you're going to go?' Alexandros demanded with rampant incredulity.

Katie opened the door. 'Back where I came from!'

In a move that took her entirely by surprise, Alexandros reached over her head with infuriating ease to flip shut the door again.

'What do you think you're playing at?' Katie whirled back to face him in a fury. 'I'm not staying here!'

'At present, there isn't a better option.'

Her green eyes shone with defiance. 'You can't make me stay—and do you want to know something? I really do wish I *had* sold that story! It's what you deserved, but I was too nicely brought up to do it. I didn't have the guts.'

'If that is true, then I would owe you an apology. But the devil is in the detail. Where did your friend get the photos?'

'Leanne is storing a lot of my stuff in her flat right now. That included those photos.'

'But there were certain facts that only you knew—'

'She was my friend…so I talked to her,' Katie said defensively.

A level ebony brow climbed. 'Yackety-yack…what happened to discretion?'

'So I'm not as inhibited as you are!'

'Who are you calling inhibited?' Alexandros planted his lean powerful frame so close that she could not turn round to reopen the door. 'You only make love in a blackout…lights off, curtains closed, sheet to throat!'

Her face aflame with furious chagrin, Katie backed up against the door. 'Get out of my way, Alexandros!'

'No. I'm thinking for both of us right now.'

Outrage shone in her flushed face. 'Tell me I didn't hear you say that—'

Alexandros rested lean brown hands either side of her head, so that she could not escape his circle of entrapment. 'I remember this like it happened yesterday,' he breathed soft and low. 'You get so mad you don't think about what you're doing—'

'And you're the insulting, scornful voice of all-knowing logic, are you?' Katie hissed, standing up on tiptoe, the better to fire back those disdainful words at him.

Alexandros gazed down at her with shimmering dark golden eyes full of molten appreciation. Her tummy flipped, and a little frisson of heat curled low in her pelvis. 'I know what you want *now*…'

Her mouth ran dry, and she felt her heart thumping a little too fast for comfort behind her breastbone. 'You just think you do. You always think you are one step ahead.'

'If I wasn't one step ahead, you'd be on the other side of that door right now.' Alexandros let his hands slowly slide down to her shoulders. It was a caressing move, and wholly confident. She quivered, green eyes welded to his with an electric anticipation that she couldn't hide. Only with her had he ever experienced that kind of non-verbal communication. It gave him the most incomparable sense of power and heightened arousal.

'Please don't…' Katie whispered shakily, stealing a quick shallow breath and fighting what she was feeling with every weapon in her armoury. She knew that she should lift her hands to push him away, but she didn't trust herself to make physical contact. Even as she held her slim body still she was extraordinarily conscious of the taut swell of her breasts and the ache of almost unbearable tension at the heart of her.

'Don't what?' Alexandros murmured, soft and low as a purring tiger, his entire concentration bent on her. 'If you want me to back off, tell me.'

His dark golden eyes were as hot and bright as strong sunlight. He knew she wasn't going to tell him to back off. Rage rose in her, but she knew it too. Her palms tingled, for she would dearly have loved to slap him for his audacity. But when she focussed on those lean, darkly handsome features, more primitive responses took precedence and made nonsense of all thought and restraint.

Alexandros smiled and her heart danced. Long brown fingers tilted up her chin and she shifted almost infinitesimally closer, her pupils dilated. He let his wide, sensual mouth graze the merest corner of hers, his breath fanning her cheek, and a faint gasp of disappointment was wrenched from her. He bent down, dropping his hands to her waist and lifting her to him with an easy strength that sent a burning river of desire snaked through her.

'*Theos mou*…I want you.'

'We can't…we mustn't,' Katie gasped as he brought her down on a sofa and leant over her.

But a hot-wire sensation that almost hurt tightened in her pelvis, and her fingers spread and speared into his black luxuriant hair. She drew him down to her, controlled by a helpless hunger that paid no heed to more sensible promptings.

He tasted her generous pink mouth with the provocative sensuality that was so much a part of him.

'I hate jeans, *pedhi mou*,' Alexandros reminded her hoarsely, skimming a censorious hand down over a slender thigh sheathed in denim.

His second kiss was slow and deep, and she shivered violently, breathing in shallow bursts. Pulling back from her with the predatory grace and assurance of a hunter who enjoyed the kill, he pushed the T-shirt she wore up out of his path and bared her narrow ribcage.

'Alexandros,' she breathed shakily, on the edge of an exhilaration so intense she was terrified.

'Your skin is very white…' Scorching golden eyes fiercely focussed, Alexandros inched up the garment that still concealed her from him. When he finally exposed the pert, rounded swell of her breasts, his attention lingered on her taut rosy nipples and a gruff little sound of masculine appreciation was drawn from him. He bent his head and employed his mouth on a single throbbing peak, and a low keening moan of pleasure was wrenched from her.

Across the room, a phone rang. 'Ignore it,' he told her thickly.

But the phone rang and rang and rang, and it had no sooner fallen silent when a few moments later a knock sounded on the door. With a splintering Greek curse on his lips, Alexandros vaulted off the sofa and raked his hand through his hair in a gesture of fierce frustration. 'Whatever you do, don't move—and don't start thinking, *pedhi mou*.'

For several seconds she lay there obediently, still ensnared by the flood of excitement he had released inside her. And then the low murmur of voices from the door at the other end of the room, allied to that suspicious injunction against thought, combined and exploded her out of her waking sensual dream with a vengeance. Hauling her clothing back into place with clumsy hands, Katie sat up and scrambled upright. She was shaking like a leaf inside and out. How could she have forgotten herself to that extent? Her heart-shaped face turned a slow painful pink. How could she have lain there, revelling in what he was making her feel, as if the past had not happened?

Lean, powerful face clenched taut, Alexandros closed the door again. 'Apparently the nanny I engaged is having trouble with Toby and Connor. I can't believe that the children can't do without you for five minutes. It may well be that my staff have hired some over-zealous nurse—'

Katie's guilt went into mega-drive. 'Where are they?'

'The housekeeper will take you to them.'

As Katie surged past him to yank open the door again, Alexandros caught her hand unexpectedly in his and wound her back to him as easily as if she had been a toy. 'Don't keep me waiting too long…'

Katie stiffened, and refused to meet his smouldering gaze. She was at the mercy of a seething discomfiture that told her she could be justly accused of blowing hot and then cold. 'I don't want anything to happen between us…okay? Been there, done that—'

'And can't wait to do it again?' Alexandros slotted in, impervious as a brick wall to that suggestion of caution and moderation.

'No, I'm serious. I don't like being in your house,' Katie

admitted tightly. 'It feels wrong. I'll feel much more comfortable somewhere on my own—'

'On your own?' Alexandros repeated drily.

'I don't belong here. I don't like being around you—'

'Correction…you like it too much.'

Katie flinched as though she had been slapped, and half turned her head away. 'The twins and I do need your help to get somewhere decent to live—'

Alexandros swore under his breath. 'If the DNA tests confirm what I already expect, do you think that finding you an apartment will be enough to satisfy me?'

'If you want to see the kids, of course you can visit… whatever…' Katie muttered, desperate to conclude the conversation. 'But that's the only contact we need to have.'

He released her hand with exaggerated immediacy. 'And that's what you want?'

'Yes.' Even as she spoke she knew she was lying. She wanted him, feared that she would always want him, that there would never be a time that she could look on his lean, dark, devastating face without feeling almost more than she could bear in silence.

Angrier than he had been in a very long time, Alexandros watched her leave. He had always appreciated the fact that she didn't play female games with him. What she said she always meant; what she promised had always been delivered. He loathed pretence. That she should deny him when he could feel her hunger in every fibre of his being infuriated him. She had to have an ulterior motive for her behaviour, he reflected grimly.

The housekeeper, a trim middle-aged woman, was waiting for Katie at the foot of the magnificent staircase. Katie felt as though she had gone ten rounds with a boxer and had staggered up after being knocked out cold. She knew how narrow her escape had been in the drawing room. Alexandros would not have hesitated to take her on the sofa, and she would never have recovered from letting herself down like that, she thought in an agony of self-reproach.

Glancing up as she climbed the stairs, she focussed on the huge oil painting of a woman on the wall above. It stirred a vague memory of a photo she had seen in Ireland and her blood ran cold. 'Who's that?' she asked abruptly.

'The late Mrs Christakis, madam.'

A stunningly beautiful ice-blonde, garbed in a magnificent blue evening gown. Mrs Christakis? Late? As in…dead? Alexandros was a widower? Having denied that he was either married or divorced, what else could he be? Her face tight and pale, Katie stared up at the portrait which now exercised the most fatal fascination over her. 'When did she die?'

'October, the year before last…a car crash in the South of France. A terrible tragedy,' her companion replied.

Katie had to literally drag her eyes from the painting and force her paralysed limbs to move her on and up the stairs. As the housekeeper spoke, her heart had sunk to her toes, and her tummy had responded with a sick lurch. Her skin felt clammy, and she realised that she had gone into shock. Perhaps her reaction was not that surprising now that she knew that she had had a passionate affair with a guy who had buried his wife only weeks before he'd met her. And he hadn't told her. In fact he had deliberately denied her that painful truth.

'Who's that?' she had asked, when she had picked up the tiny photo from the floor in his office.

'Nobody important,' he had asserted.

No, just his wife. Whom he had married when he was barely out of his teens, according to the *Globe*. Of course he hadn't wanted to talk about her, and when she had looked again later there had been no sign of the photo. She hadn't thought anything of the fact. Incredibly, innocently happy as she had been with Alexandros that winter, she had not been at all suspicious of anything he said or did.

But in retrospect it was as if she had suddenly been handed the missing piece of a jigsaw that she had somehow previously believed complete when it was not. Alexandros had come to Ireland and locked himself away in that remote and beautiful house because he had been grieving. Hadn't she seen that brooding sadness and anger in him? She had simply assumed that he was some high-flying business executive suffering from burn-out after working excessive hours. The actual truth was far less welcome.

Toby and Connor's wails provided only the briefest respite from her unhappy thoughts. The anxious nanny looked on with relief when the babies calmed down as soon as their youthful mother reappeared. Katie sat on the carpet with a twin settled on either thigh and held them close. As she breathed in her sons' warm familiar scent, and kissed first one dark head and then the other, she was hiding the reality that her own face was wet with tears.

Her affair with Alexandros and its abrupt and cruel conclusion now made much more sense to her. She had offered comfort of the most basic variety. He was a very physical, very passionate guy. He hadn't wanted to tell her about his wife or talk about his loss, and that said so much, didn't it? That loss would have gone very deep; he had married young and shared his life for a good decade with Ianthe.

Had he felt guilty about sleeping with Katie within weeks of that tragedy? No doubt that was why Alexandros had been so keen to eradicate her from his life again. She had been the living, breathing adult equivalent of a hot water bottle or a soothing teddy bear. Just a source of physical relief. Acknowledging that hurt Katie a great deal, and made her all the more aware that living in the radius of Alexandros Christakis was very bad for her self-esteem.

When she had started working for him in Ireland she had found him impossible to please. From the first day he had made her feel as though her very presence below the same roof during the hours of daylight was an irritant. At first he had barely spoken, but his impatience, exacting standards and exasperation had soon cleared that barrier. Everything she'd done had seemed to annoy him. He had requested dishes she didn't know how to cook and had rejected her best efforts. By the end of the first week he had rebuked her for being too talkative, for being late, noisy and disorganised, and had also contrived to imply that she was guilty of chatting up the delivery men. She had gone from fancying the socks off Alexandros and standing breathless in his presence to hating him with such roaring virulence that she had positively boiled with her sense of injustice

'What an achievement… That tastes even more poisonous than it looks,' he had commented silkily on the sixth day, thrusting away the meal she had presented him with.

And as Katie had loaded the rejected dish back onto the tray and turned away, she'd suddenly totally lost the rag with him and had spun back to pitch the entire tray down at his feet. 'You are the most obnoxious guy I've ever met!' she'd launched at him. 'Nothing I do is good enough for you!'

'So you try to assault me?'

'If I assaulted you, you'd know about it!'

Alexandros had surveyed her with icy dark affront and censure, and told her that she was sacked.

She had stalked out of the house, and as she'd cycled down that endless lane, dismounting to get through every successive gate, her anger had soon ebbed, to be replaced by growing dismay and regret. After all, the job she'd sacrificed was actually her mother's, and it was her mother's reputation and references that would suffer, not her own. Appalled that she had let anger overpower all judgement, she had returned to the house.

'No…' Alexandros had delivered, the instant she'd attempted to apologise. 'You have no discipline, and you're not up to the duties involved.'

'I could learn—'

'You've got the wrong attitude.'

'I'm willing to grovel.'

A level dark brow had elevated. 'I will not tolerate or forgive impertinence or incompetence.'

'Please don't report this to the agency.' Seeing no point in continuing the pretence that she was her mother, Katie had made a full confession on that score and had had to admit that her only previous experience lay in an office environment.

'You amaze me…you confess to barefaced lying and expect to be re-employed?'

'I'll change my attitude and cook stuff you like…any time you like,' Katie had proffered in desperation, green eyes connecting with burnished gold, her heart starting to race without any warning. 'Give me another chance and I'll do whatever you ask me.'

'Bring me breakfast in bed? Wear skirts instead of jeans?'

Her eyes had opened very wide in surprise.

'I didn't say that,' Alexandros had asserted in hasty retraction, his stunning gaze narrowed, very bright and almost defensive. 'But certain offers are open to misinterpretation.'

And that was when it had finally dawned on her that the aggression in the air between her and the aloof Greek might well stem from an attraction that they were both determined to suppress.

'I should not have said that.'

'But you did…' Suddenly maddeningly aware of the way his intent gaze was welded to hers, Katie had laughed, feeling dizzy with a wanton sense of achievement that was new to her.

'Don't flirt with me,' Alexandros had told her.

Compressing her lips, she'd nodded, bowed her head and regarded him from below her lashes.

'Even the way you look at me is provocative.'

Face flaming, Katie had closed her eyes tight.

'Try to act normally,' Alexandros had urged gently.

Eyes opening a chink, she'd nodded vigorously.

The helicopter, which made regular deliveries, had come the next day, and, solemn as a judge, Alexandros had presented her with a Greek recipe book. She'd had to ask him to translate the recipe she chose. He'd stayed to watch her cook, and had invited her to eat with him. Barrier after barrier had come down at breathtaking speed. He'd no longer ignored her. He'd begun to smile and respond a tad stiffly to her conversational sallies. Within forty-eight hours she'd been walking on air and had abandoned all caution. It was that same week that a male childhood friend of her mother's had flown in from New Zealand for a long vacation. Blossoming beneath daily visits that had soon evolved into a determined courtship, Maura Fletcher had been too preoccupied to notice the increasing irregularity of her daughter's working hours.

The third week Katie had started wearing skirts, and Alexandros had accused her of flirting with the gardener, who had been old enough to be her father. In the ensuing argument, during which Katie had threatened to resign,

Alexandros had called her a tease and hauled her into his arms and kissed her. He'd kept on kissing her all the way upstairs to his bed. That reckless conflagration of passion had plunged them into an affair without any boundaries whatsoever. Nothing they had shared had been discussed or decided in the weeks that followed.

Lying sleepless in her beautiful bedroom in Alexandros's fabulous country house, Katie came back to the present with an even stronger conviction that she had to protect herself from being hurt a second time. She had lunched with the twins, taken them out for a long walk that afternoon, and dined alone. She could not forget how she had once sunk without trace in the intensity of her feelings for Alexandros. Holding nothing back, she had closed her eyes to every warning sign and just revelled in adoring him. She had never loved like that before, had in truth never even grasped what temptation was until she had succumbed to it without the smallest struggle. Although a healthy number of young men had shown interest in Katie at university, they had almost all left her physically cold. The only one who hadn't had bruised her heart and her ego by swiftly bedding someone else when she'd proved to be too much of a challenge. Now she wondered fearfully if she was the sort of misguided female who only really fell for the guys who wanted her least...

The next morning, Alexandros surveyed the single sheet of paper. He was not surprised by the DNA test results. The 99.9999% result tallied exactly with his gloomiest expectations. He was the father of the two little boys currently occupying the nursery on the top floor.

His private line buzzed. He swept up the receiver, his lean dark face clenching hard when he recognised his grandfather's unusually low-pitched voice. He breathed in deep. 'The children are mine,' he confirmed.

'How do you feel?' Pelias Christakis enquired, in an upbeat encouraging tone that disconcerted Alexandros—until he worked out that the older man had to be masking his true reactions out of affection for him.

'How I feel doesn't come into it,' Alexandros responded flatly.

'It must be fate,' his grandfather informed him without hesitation. 'You said you would have no children but… here they are.'

Alexandros gritted his teeth at that untimely reminder, and offered to fly out so that he could break the news to his grandmother. The older man said that he would prefer to perform that task himself. Alexandros salved his guilty conscience with the assurance that he would marry the twins' mother as soon as it could be arranged.

In answer, Pelias released a heavy sigh.

Katie had just finished bathing Toby and Connor when she received the message that Alexandros was waiting for her in the library. In the act of returning to her bedroom to tidy herself, she froze. Her face was pink, her hair was tumbled and she was clad in jeans and a T-shirt—but did that matter? she asked herself staunchly. She needed to learn to look on Alexandros as simply Toby and Connor's father, and suppress any more personal sense of connection. In any case, she could fuss the rest of the morning and it would make precious little difference when she had no make-up, no smart clothes and her hair badly needed a trim.

On the way downstairs, her sons left in the care of the nanny, Katie did wonder why Alexandros kept on hauling her into a clinch? Was he just oversexed? At a loss as to how else to relate to her? She focussed on the portrait of the exquisite Ianthe and glanced hurriedly away again, stifling a pang of envy that made her feel ashamed. But there was no comparison between them. Ianthe had been Greek, rich and classically beautiful, *and* the love of her husband's life. Katie discovered that she did not even want to look in the direction of that painting, which seemed to stand for everything that she herself was not and made her feel very small, cheap and forgettable.

Alexandros swung round from the window when she entered. Immaculate in a charcoal-grey business suit and a snazzy red and grey striped silk tie, the impact of his lithe bronzed male beauty punched a hole through her defensive shell.

'You have to be the most invisible guest I believe I've ever had,' he murmured, his attention nailed to her triangular face while he tried to work out how she could look so good without the artifice of cosmetics. 'I have not laid eyes on you since yesterday.'

Katie shot him a winging glance and swiftly veiled her gaze. But she still saw his image in her mind's eye, and he took her breath away. The armoured indifference she longed to achieve was still a long way from fruition. 'It's a big house.'

'Before I forget, I want you to authorise the removal of your possessions from the place where you were staying. The items you had stored at your former friend's apartment should also be collected.'

'Of course.' Hurt by that inadvertent reminder of Leanne's betrayal, Katie paled.

'Would you like coffee?' Alexandros enquired, coolly polite once the details of those arrangements had been spelled out.

'No, thanks.'

'Take a seat. What I have to say will take some time.'

Katie folded obediently down on to the edge of an antique armchair and studied his desk rather than him.

'The DNA tests confirm that the boys are mine.'

Her cheeks reddened.

'No comment?'

'What do you want me to say? The tests were offensive, but pretty much what I expected from you.'

Alexandros tensed. 'How…offensive?'

'You know when Toby and Connor were born, and you know you were the first guy I slept with. I fell pregnant the first week we were together,' Katie reminded him tightly as she stared into space. 'Another contender in the paternity corner wasn't very likely.'

Almost imperceptible colour demarcated his superb cheekbones. 'I had to be sure. I take nothing at face value.'

'Especially bad news.'

'Katie…that kind of comment is counter-productive at this stage. Naturally this development has come as a surprise, but I will adjust to it.' Alexandros contemplated the rounded swell of her small breasts below the cotton top, and wondered if it was a flesh-coloured bra or skin that he could see beneath.

'But you don't need to adjust to anything.' Uneasily conscious of his masculinity, Katie raked a restive hand through her tousled copper tresses and jerked a thin shoulder in dismissive emphasis. 'Nothing has to change in your life. I'm not looking for a father for the twins.'

It was a bra, not skin, Alexandros registered in some disappointment when she moved. He emitted a sardonic laugh that struck her as distinctly unamused. 'Very funny…'

Her green eyes gleamed. 'I wasn't trying to be funny. Just fair and honest—'

'How very considerate of you,' Alexandros breathed with scarcely leashed impatience, forcing his attention to a level above her head while he questioned the juvenile fascination he had with her skinny little body. 'But I should not need to state that I fully intend to be a father to my own sons. That is a duty I will not take lightly.'

His unemotional choice of words stung Katie's pride and stirred her into anger. She was tempted to tell him that as long as Toby and Connor had her love they would all manage very well without his dutiful input. 'I'm not sure I want you to act as a role model for the twins.'

Alexandros dealt her an icy glance. 'What reason have you to insult me?'

A mutinous expression on her heart-shaped face, Katie tore her gaze from the shimmering golden challenge of his and dropped her head. She bit back further hasty words, regretting her lack of control over her own tongue. It would be madness to make their relationship a hostile one, she reminded herself ruefully. 'I'm sorry...I didn't mean to offend you.'

'Evidently it has not yet occurred to you that I'm prepared to *marry* you and provide the perfect role-model for my sons!' Alexandros spoke with a harsh emphasis that clarified his attitude towards that prospect better than any words could have done.

Shock reverberating through her slight taut figure, Katie blinked and stared fixedly at him. 'You're prepared to marry me? At this moment you're *asking* me to marry you?'

Alexandros released his breath in an exasperated hiss. 'What else did you expect from me?'

All of a sudden the reason for his bleak and sardonic mood became clear to Katie. Even though the angry flush in her cheeks had receded, she was if anything more furious with him than ever. A hollow sense of pain settled like a stone inside her. She imagined that when he had proposed to Ianthe, the late lost love of his life, the scenario, the atmosphere and the emotions involved would all have been very different. 'Well, I didn't expect your grudging proposal, and I'm not grateful for it either!' she countered, with a defiant rise in volume. 'Thankfully, there's no need for either of us to make such a horrible sacrifice of ourselves.'

'There is every need. The twins should have two parents.'

Humiliation writhed inside Katie like a wild thing. She wanted to sob with rage and hurt. 'I don't even like you…and I certainly wouldn't want to marry you purely for my children's sake!'

Alexandros surveyed her with scorching eyes of gold, his stubborn jawline squaring. There she sat, all five-foot-nothing of her, being bloody cheeky, feminine and infuriating. Of course she would marry him! For her to pretend otherwise was nonsense. 'You don't feel like that.'

'Don't tell me how I feel—'

'I probably have a better grasp of how you feel than you do. Why are you so angry with me? Here I am, ready and willing to do the decent thing and make you my wife!' Alexandros threw up lean brown hands in a gesture that encompassed his opinion of the sheer magnificence of that offer.

Loathing leapt up like a core of steel within Katie's anger. *The decent thing?* She shook her copper head in vehement refusal. 'Luckily for both of us, I'm not that desperate, greedy or stupid. We have nothing in common but the twins—'

'Sex,' Alexandros slotted in, without a shade of discomfiture. If he was doomed to live with an adolescent preoccupation with her body, marriage would at least provide an ample outlet for it.

Katie was mortified by that bold and earthy reminder of her weakness. 'We'd need something rather more than that to make a marriage.'

Alexandros dealt her a sincerely enquiring glance. 'Such as what?'

Katie was momentarily stunned by the obvious fact that Alexandros appeared to rate sex as the most important element of marriage. Acknowledging that she was out of her depth, she decided not to pursue that controversial angle. 'Look, feeling as I do right now, nothing would persuade me to marry you.'

Alexandros contrived to look exceedingly unimpressed by that declaration. 'I could persuade you to share my bed again in the space of a minute.'

Katie leapt upright, her fair complexion aflame with chagrined colour, for she really could have done without that mortifying reminder. '*So*…what does that prove?' she challenged, in defiance of her own embarrassment. 'That it's been a long time since there was a man in my life?'

Alexandros frowned. 'Don't talk like that…it cheapens you. I don't like it.'

Katie twisted her head away, fighting for control. He had been the only man, and that awareness rankled. While he had entertained himself with a succession of supermodels her life had fallen apart, destroyed first by pregnancy, then by motherhood and lack of cash. All of a sudden she could no longer silence her strong sense of injustice. 'I really don't care what you like. I'm only twenty-three years old. You are so precious about your privacy, your reputation, *your* life! What about mine?' she demanded wrathfully.

'Meaning?' Alexandros queried, with the weary aspect of a guy forced to humour a hysteric.

'Do you think this is the life that I wanted or would have

chosen? I didn't want to become a mother at my age. And I don't feel like getting married either,' she confessed shakily. 'I want to go out clubbing again. I want to date. I want my single life back!'

CHAPTER FIVE

HUGELY taken aback by Katie's startling confession of intent, Alexandros discovered that he had to call on every atom of self-discipline to keep his temper. He was astonished that his proposal had met with a negative response.

Surely she recognised that the twins' future security and their rights of inheritance could only be safeguarded by their marriage? It was the practical solution, and he was a practical guy. He knew what he owed his children, even if she did not. His family were very conservative, and took certain conventions for granted. His irresponsible father might have flouted those principles, but Alexandros had made it his mission to live within them.

He regarded Katie with smouldering force, an aggressive current that was unfamiliar to him blurring his usually ice-cool thoughts. She wanted her single life back? What the hell was that supposed to mean? Running about with other guys? Sleeping around? If she had hoped to pack in that kind of experience, she should have taken care of it before she'd met him, because now it was out of the question. Of course it was out of the question, when the only male she had ever slept with was him. His level ebony brows pleated while he tried to work out why the suggestion that she might get into another man's bed should outrage him to such an extent.

Theos mou, she was the mother of his children, and that was reason enough! That put her into a very special, indeed unique category, he reasoned fiercely. She wasn't entitled to a single life. But perhaps now was not the moment to spell out that inescapable truth, for his legal counsel had already warned him that unmarried fathers had very few rights within the law. For the first time he appreciated that marriage would bring advantages other than sexual. He would gain control over her *and* his sons.

Registering that she was trembling, and that her eyes were full of stinging tears, Katie walked jerkily over to the window and turned a defensive back on him. She wrapped her arms round herself and fought to get a grip on her flailing emotions. How dared he look so shocked! Did he think no other man would ever look at her? How dared he think that she would marry a guy who was only asking her out of a sense of obligation? Catch her accepting the role of a poor second best to the love of his life! Catch her saddling a reluctant father with children he had no interest in!

'I don't feel right staying here. Please find me somewhere else to go as soon as possible,' Katie muttered uncomfortably, her delicate profile taut. 'Then we can both get on with our lives.'

Alexandros stilled, anger cooled by an instant warning jab of disquiet. He realised that it was time for the creative thinking at which he excelled in finance. Her hostility and her desire for independence disconcerted him, because he knew it was essential that he keep her on board and engage in dialogue. Perhaps what was required was a breathing spell in a more relaxed environment. 'I think we can do better than that,' he asserted smoothly. 'I have a speech to give in Rome tonight. Why don't you fly out the day after tomorrow and join me at my home in Italy for a few days?'

Taken utterly by surprise at that suggestion, Katie could not conceal her confusion. 'I…well—'

'We need time and space to talk our options over…as friends, if nothing else.'

A faint flush of discomfiture warmed Katie's cheeks when she discovered that her immediate reaction to that suggestion of friendship was one of recoil. She did not want Alexandros as a friend, yet she knew that she ought to be relieved by that sensible offer. Her every instinct was now at war. She was even irked by the speed with which he had abandoned his talk of marrying her, and could not credit how contrary she was being.

'You'd love the sunshine,' Alexandros remarked casually. 'The twins would enjoy it too.'

'Yes…all right.' Katie was reluctantly impressed by that angle, immediately gripped by the fear that only a cruel mother would deny Toby and Connor such a treat.

'Would you mind if I spent some time with the children now?' Alexandros knew to quit while he was ahead. But he was remembering again: Katie rushing outdoors in Ireland to rejoice in a pitiful patch of wintry sunlight, telling him cheerfully about the excitement of her one and only trip abroad. He had been touched by her happy recollection of a childhood which had struck him as wretchedly impoverished.

'Of course not…'

His formality set her at a distance. As she accompanied him upstairs, he asked if the provisions made for the twins were acceptable.

'More than acceptable.' Katie raised a speaking brow, because the nanny was experienced and the nursery was full of designer baby equipment and toys.

'The nanny is, of course, only temporary. My staff are already drawing up a shortlist of more permanent options. You may make the final selection,' he advised. 'I've also made financial arrangements to cover your needs and that of the children in the short term—'

Katie stiffened. '*My* needs? But you only have to worry about Toby and Connor's.'

'If my sons are to live in comfort, so must you. To do so, you will require adequate funding,' Alexandros countered. 'You'll have to accept a personal allowance from me above and beyond the children's expenses.'

'I couldn't possibly—'

'I can't see that you have a choice. Obviously you've gone without many things, but there is no longer any need for such self-sacrifice. You need clothes.'

That blunt comment silenced Katie, because she was embarrassed by the fact that he'd noticed that all she owned was jeans and casual tops.

'I'll see that you're taken out shopping tomorrow. The children require clothing as well.'

When Alexandros entered the nursery, Toby and Connor displayed instant interest at his appearance. Indeed, Toby hauled himself up to stand on wobbling legs using the cot bars, his little face lighting up with a huge smile as he raised his arms to be lifted. When, without the support of the cot rail, he then fell over on his bottom the affront to his expectations was too great, and he burst into angry tears of frustration.

Katie was disconcerted when Alexandros strode straight over and scooped Toby up into his arms, voicing what sounded like a sympathetic phrase of Greek. In the space of a minute Toby went from tears to delighted chortles. Equally confused by his own behaviour, Alexandros gazed down at his son, marvelling that some hitherto unknown instinct should have prompted him to immediately offer comfort to the distressed child.

In search of an equal share of the attention, Connor loosed a plaintive yell. Katie lifted him, but Connor was much more interested in Alexandros. The twins were used to women, and a man was an infinitely greater source of fascination. Her face tightened and she stifled an ignoble spark of hurt when Connor stretched out eager hands in his father's direction.

'They're very friendly babies.' Alexandros, gloriously unaware of the compliment he was being paid, was amused. 'But I'll have to sit down to handle the two of them.'

When Alexandros sank down with lithe grace on to the carpet, Katie set Connor down beside him. The little boy hauled himself upright on a hard male thigh and chuckled with satisfaction. Katie watched in wonderment while the twins swarmed over their father with increasing confidence and pleasure. They tried to use his tie as a climbing rope. They clutched at his hair, explored his face with highly familiar fingers, and were overjoyed when he responded with more excitingly physical and challenging moves than their mother ever did.

For the first time since the twins' birth Katie was ignored by her children. As Toby and Connor crawled round, staging frantic sneak attacks on Alexandros, and the minutes ticked past while the audible sounds of their enjoyment rang round the room, Katie felt that she might as well have been the invisible woman. It had never occurred to her that Alexandros would or even *could* unbend from his reserve and his dignity to such an extent.

Cyrus came to remind Alexandros that he would soon have to leave for the airport. His craggy features betrayed his surprise at finding his sophisticated employer engaging in a baby wrestling match, and his beaming approval of the scene was equally obvious.

'Your suit is going to look like you slept in it,' Katie told Alexandros waspishly.

He raked long brown fingers through his tousled black hair and shot her a sudden charismatic grin, his amusement unhidden. 'I don't think I've had this much fun since I left my own nursery…all boys together, rough and tumble.'

Striving to remain impervious to that lethally attractive smile, Katie folded her arms. 'Toby and Connor can be quite difficult to handle.'

Alexandros vaulted easily upright and shrugged, dismissing her negative comment. 'They like me. That's a good beginning.'

'Yes.' Feeling small and mean and jealous, she tried to inject more enthusiasm into her voice.

The twins cried bitterly when the games stopped and their father departed. Settling them again took time.

That afternoon, Katie was invited to sit in on the nanny interviews. Invited to give her opinion afterwards, she gave her vote to a French girl called Maribel, who was the youngest applicant and whom Katie had found the least intimidating.

The next day, Cyrus and another security man accompanied Katie to Harrods. Assisted by a personal shopper, she bought new clothes for her sons. Not having to worry about the price tags was a wonderfully liberating experience. Then she tried on a variety of outfits for herself, and chose the accessories that went with them. By the time she reached the stage of selecting underwear and nightwear, she felt like an overexcited child let loose in a toy shop.

When the chauffeur went to stow the bags and boxes in the vast boot of the limo, she asked if they could be placed in the back seat with her. She spent the entire drive home carefully examining every purchase and soaking up every last possible thrill from the experience. It was only fair that Alexandros should contribute to the cost of keeping the twins clothed, but she was determined that this would be the only time when she allowed him to include her in that responsibility. In the future she planned to be working and earning and fully self-sufficient.

Walking back into the house, Katie glimpsed her reflection in a mirror and fingered her undisciplined mop of curls in dismay. 'I should've got my hair done…I forgot about it.'

'I'll organise it,' Cyrus told her.

That evening she visited a beauty salon, where her hair was styled and her nails were manicured. She chose some cosmetics as well, and at midnight she was still experimenting with the eye make-up. In bed, she lay as still as a corpse, her mane of ringlets carefully spread in separate lengths across the pillow, her hands, with fuchsia-pink-tinted perfect nails, spread like starfish on top of the duvet. There was nothing wrong with taking pride in her appearance, she told herself, in conflict with the puritanical inner voice that suggested that she was being foolish. Just because Alexandros had been married to a woman with the face and body of a goddess did not mean that she herself had to give up entirely. In any case, she and Alexandros would meet as friends in Italy. It would be a new chapter in their relationship, a more mature and civilised phase, she reminded herself drowsily, wondering why being sensible should make her feel so unbearably sad…

As the car wended a slow path, first through an enchantingly pretty medieval village and then down a steep hill into a valley with a meandering river that glinted in the sunlight like a silver ribbon, Katie was delighted with her first impressions of Italy. It was hot and sunny, and the Umbrian countryside was glorious.

Beside her, Toby and Connor were mercifully quiet. The twins were teething, and after a restless night had been in no mood to embrace foreign travel. The disruption to their usual routine had been unwelcome, and the boys had complained vociferously during the flight. Katie hoped that an uninterrupted nap when they arrived at their destination would help her sons catch up on the sleep they had missed out on.

The limo purred up a formal avenue towards a vast villa that looked as if it had been around for centuries, and Katie could not resist a rueful grin. Alexandros had never seemed quite comfortable in the ultra-modern house in Ireland. Classical grandeur, however, provided him with a perfect backdrop. As she entered the villa, she was handed a phone.

'Will you join me for lunch?' Alexandros enquired.

An instant smile curved her generous mouth, for she had been disappointed that he wasn't on the spot to greet them. 'I'd love to…but I do have to get the twins settled first—'

Overhearing that declaration, the new nanny, Maribel, made frantic signs to indicate that there was no need whatsoever for Katie to join her in that endeavour.

'Oh—no…no, it's okay. I can come now.' Katie returned her attention to the phone. 'Where are you?'

'The car will bring you to me.'

The limo moved off again, and turned slowly down a cobbled lane overhung by trees. Katie smoothed damp palms down over her summer dress, a simple but madly fashionable item composed of fine lilac-sprigged organza and shaped with ribbon below the bust. A few minutes later the car came to a halt, and she slid out.

Alexandros strolled out from below an ivy-clad arched gateway. He wore a slate-grey designer suit, casually cut and teamed with a striped black shirt. He exuded cool cutting-edge style. Katie tried not to be dazzled, and struggled to suppress her usual response to his sleek, dark good-looks. Friends, she repeated inwardly. Even so, her mouth still ran dry, and it was as steep a challenge as ever to dredge her attention from his lean bronzed features.

'Today will mark a new beginning for us…'

Katie moistened her lower lip in a nervous gesture 'Yes…'

Coal-black lashes low over his stunning golden eyes, Alexandros studied her luscious pink mouth with ferocious intensity. He could not understand how she should look so wildly sexy in a dress that concealed her slender curves and showed only a modest length of leg. He could not understand either how he had dismissed her attractions just a few days earlier and yet now burned to get her back into bed again by whatever stratagems necessary. Perhaps, he acknowledged, his strong reaction was magnified by the simple fact that he had never been so focussed on a woman before.

From the moment when it had occurred to Alexandros that his staying single meant Katie stayed single too—with all the freedom and all the choices that status entailed—he had seen the need for aggressive action. Unlike with most of the young women Alexandros met, the acquisition of a rich husband was definitely not the summit of Katie's ambition. Katie didn't *want* to marry him. That revelation had challenged him as never before, rousing hunting instincts that had stayed dormant because he had never had to chase a woman. So he had plotted Katie's downfall with the same ruthless and resolute precision with which he made financial deals. Romance? Success came easily to Alexandros in every field, and he saw no reason why he should not be able to do romance as well as he did everything else. And he had baited the trap with care.

Katie was captivated by her first glimpse of the turreted stone folly through the trees. The winding woodland path petered out into a lush green glade. A glorious rose-entwined loggia rimmed the lower floor of the tower. She fell still under the shade of a chestnut tree, to better appreciate the sheer quality of the scene before her. On the terrace below the climbing roses sat elegant ironwork chairs, festooned with colourful floral quilts and silk cushions, and a white marble table which was a work of art: glittering crystal glasses, delicate silver and glass dishes, offering a mouthwatering selection of finger foods.

Kicking off her shoes, Katie let her toes flex in the springy grass and kept on staring. For perhaps the very first time she was truly appreciating how very rich Alexandros was. An *al fresco* lunch was being offered in an exquisite theatrical display worthy of a glossy magazine spread.

'This is out of this world…' Katie whispered. 'But you don't like eating outdoors—'

'And you do.'

'Since when did you put what *I* liked ahead of what *you* liked?' Katie asked, genuinely not trying to score a point, just saying it as it was.

'I try to do something thoughtful and kind and you want to argue about it?' Alexandros chided in his rich dark drawl.

Guilty pink mantled Katie's cheeks

'Naturally I knew that you would enjoy this sort of thing.' The gesture of a lean brown hand encompassed the superb picnic scene. 'My sole objective was to please.'

'It's just beautiful.' Embarrassed by the tactlessness that had made her sound more critical than appreciative, Katie got very busy spreading a couple of quilts on the grass and dropping cushions in rather pointless heaps here and there.

Alexandros shed his jacket, lounged back against the table and poured the wine. Katie drank with more thirst than delicacy, for even below the wide canopy of the chestnut tree she was warm. She sat down on a quilt and contemplated the ancient tower. 'Was it built just to embellish the woods, or did someone actually live in it once?'

Alexandros spun out an ironwork chair for her occupation. 'The *palazzo* was built by a nobleman in the sixteenth century. He kept his mistress in the tower.'

Relaxed on the quilt, Katie ignored the invitation to eat at the table. 'Was he married?'

Releasing the chair with an acknowledgement that the informality of the quilt would work to his advantage, Alexandros sent her an amused glance. Sometimes her innocence made him want to laugh out loud, but he did not want to hurt her feelings. He offered her a plate of canapés and refreshed her wine glass. 'I've never thought about it, but I expect so…'

'A wife and a mistress within walking distance…' Katie veiled her gaze, his gorgeous image imprinted on her senses like a brand. She was tempted to quip that she was sure that he would behave no better were he to marry purely out of a sense of duty. She wanted so badly to ask him about Ianthe, but resisted the urge as he had made it plain that that was a conversational no-go area. That exclusion hurt, reminding her when she did not need reminding that she had no proper status in his world.

Alexandros settled down beside her with the predatory grace of movement that had always attracted her attention. She made herself look away while he asked her about the twins and the flight. As she talked, her nervous tension ebbed and she relaxed, basking in the dappled sunshine piercing the leaves above her. The heat had stolen her appetite, and she felt a little light-headed from the wine.

'It's so beautiful here—but I suppose you take it for granted because you were born to all this '

'But I *wasn't* born to it,' Alexandros murmured flatly. 'My grandparents took me in when I was six years old, and adopted me two years later.'

Thunderstruck by that admission, Katie stared at him.

'My parents weren't married. I was the result of a one-night stand,' Alexandros extended wryly. 'My mother was a flight attendant on the family jet at the time. She got into drugs when I was a toddler, and died when I was five. I was in foster care when my grandfather, Pelias, learned of my existence.'

Katie was aghast at what she was hearing. 'Didn't your father do anything?'

Alexandros shrugged. 'He never acknowledged me or helped my mother. He was a waste of space. My grandparents spent their lives clearing up after him. He died in a skiing accident when I was ten.'

'I'm sorry…' Her eyes were stinging with tears. She felt so guilty for the false assumptions she had made about his privileged beginnings. Her heart was wrenched by the reality that in his earliest years he had been denied the love and security that every young child deserved.

Alexandros watched her fighting back her tears in silent wonderment at the depth of her sympathy for the child he had long since left behind. He had found her weeping over a children's cartoon fairytale once, and had been fascinated by the tender-hearted emotionalism that went hand in hand with her hot temper. Fascinated—and then appalled—he acknowledged, swiftly burying the memory again. 'I survived,' he said lightly. 'You look delectable in that dress, *pedhi mou*.'

That change of subject and mood totally threw Katie off balance. She blinked. Belatedly aware of Alexandros's gleaming golden appraisal with every fibre in her slender body, she felt her face warm and her heart-rate speed up. Her fingers tightened round her glass, as if it was a lifebelt and she was in danger of drowning. 'I think I'd like another drink…'

Alexandros removed the goblet from her grasp. 'Sorry— when you haven't eaten much, two glasses is your limit.'

'I beg your pardon?' Katie gasped.

'Three glasses make you giggle and crack chicken-crossing-the-road jokes,' Alexandros reminded her without hesitation. 'Four make you wiggle your booty and get on my lap. And that much encouragement could be dangerous.'

That mocking recollection of her behaviour at a certain lunch back in Ireland made Katie flush to her hair-roots. Her defences were blown wide open by that mortifying reminder. 'I really acted the idiot!'

Laughing softly, Alexandros ran a light fingertip along her collarbone in a soothing gesture. 'You always go for the bait. I was only teasing you.'

Casual and brief though his touch had been, it left Katie phenomenally short of breath. 'I wasn't used to drinking wine.'

'I thought you were very natural and sexy. But I suppose I shouldn't be telling you that now.'

Starved of such compliments, Katie was hanging on his every word, disbelieving what he was saying but still revelling in it. The entire dialogue had suddenly taken on the tantalising tones of the forbidden, and she tried hard not to succumb to that lure. 'No, you shouldn't…isn't there someone else in your life?'

'There would've been, but I wanted you more,' Alexandros admitted without hesitation.

In the act of admiring the stunning symmetry of his lean bronzed features, her green eyes collided with the smouldering gold of his. Framed by black spiky lashes, his gaze was a potent weapon. Her heart was already beating so rapidly that she was scared she might be on the brink of a panic attack, and his honesty touched something deep inside her.

Alexandros had almost stopped breathing as well, and the discovery shook him. Almost as quickly, however, the fierce surge of sexual arousal took precedence over the soul-searching that was anathema to him. With unhurried cool and single-minded purpose he laced his fingers into the tumbling mass of ringlets trailing over one slight shoulder and tilted her face up to his.

'I want to kiss you, *thespinis mou*,' he told her huskily.

Say no, a little voice urged inside her head. *Say no*. She was rigid with tension and yet astonishingly aware of the tingling sensitivity of her breasts, the warm sense of melted honey pooling in the pit of her stomach. She felt insanely alive and reckless at one and the same time.

'One kiss,' Alexandros murmured, soft and low, his earthy appraisal full of masculine power and energy.

Katie trembled, knowing it would not stop at one kiss, knowing she would want it to go further. She hated herself, but his aura of sizzling sensuality held her tighter than any chains and tormented her with her weakness. 'But we—'

'Burn for one other.' Alexandros bent his darkly handsome head slowly, as if he had all the time in the world. Even then he did not do what she expected. Tugging her head back, his hand firm in her coppery mane of hair, he let his firm sensuous mouth forge a delicate trail across her collarbone, skim up the length of her satin-smooth throat and nip at the tender skin below one small ear.

By the time he went for the parted invitation of her soft pink lips she was shivering and clinging to his broad shoulders for support...

CHAPTER SIX

'*THEOS MOU*…this feels good.' Alexandros savoured, then dipped his tongue into Katie's mouth, with a provocative slide-and-thrust motion that sent shivers through her slight frame and reduced her to mental rubble.

Breathless and weak from the devastating expertise of his kisses, Katie made a feverish stab at recovery. 'We should be talking…'

Convinced that that kind of conversation would come between him and the sating of a lust which felt ungovernably strong, Alexandros tumbled her back amongst the cushions and pinned her beneath his long, powerful length. His entire concentration was welded to the concept of giving her so much pleasure that serious discussion would be the last thing on her mind, and he subjected her pouting pink mouth to the sensual exploration of his lips, teeth and tongue.

A seductive tide of pure eroticism engulfed Katie, like a flame-thrower aimed at a sheet of paper. She crackled, burned, blazed white-hot. Her hands moved in restive circles over his broad shoulders and back as the twist of restive heat in her pelvis flamed higher. Frustrated by the barrier of his shirt, she began to tug at the fabric. Levering himself back from her, Alexandros flipped loose the buttons, exposing a muscular segment of bronzed, hair-roughened chest.

Katie sucked in an unsteady breath. He was gorgeous, absolutely gorgeous, and even more perfect than she remembered. Without thought, driven by a desire she had believed she would never feel again, she came up on her knees and let her hands skim with splayed fingers over the strong wall of his rippling pectoral muscles, down to the lean hard slab of his belly. As his big powerful frame was racked by a shudder of very physical response, she was shaken by her own boldness. He peeled off the shirt and tossed it aside.

'Why would we want to talk when we can do this?' Alexandros growled, his Greek accent so thick that she could hardly distinguish the individual words. He brought both her hands back to his sleek bronzed body with the uninhibited sexuality that was the flipside of his cool, controlled nature.

'Alexandros...' Touching his warm tawny skin, she felt weak and hot with longing. He shifted against her so that her fingers trailed through the fine silky furrow of hair that arrowed down beneath his belt.

'Touch me,' he urged, closing his hands to the soft swell of her hips to crush her against him, letting her feel the blatant hardness of his arousal beneath the confining cloth at his groin.

'We shouldn't...we mustn't,' she framed dizzily, fighting the reckless swirl of reckless desire he had ignited.

But even as she spoke her slender body was already acting in direct betrayal of that bemused protest. She was locked to him, revelling in his virile heat, rejoicing in his strength and masculinity. When he crushed her reddened mouth hungrily beneath his, she moaned helplessly and let her head fall back, achingly conscious of the wanton throb at the hidden centre of her body.

Her dress dropped into a silky heap round her knees, and she surfaced from the fevered oblivion that had engulfed her with a gasp of surprise.

'We must…' His lean strong face taut, Alexandros was wholly absorbed in the fetching picture she made with her delicate curves enhanced by lace-trimmed lingerie.

Katie was entrapped by the unhidden appreciation in his glittering golden gaze. Although shy colour blossomed in her cheeks, she could not help but be thrilled that he should think her worthy of such admiration.

With a single finger he unclipped the front fastener on her bra, and the cups parted to reveal the delicate pink pouting peaks of her breasts.

'I don't know what it is about your body,' Alexandros confided thickly, as he hauled her to him with more haste than ceremony, 'but it blows me away, *glikia mou.*'

The erotic caress of his mouth on her sensitive breasts brought down any remaining barriers. As he vaulted up and lifted her into his arms she was quivering with the intensity of her response. He strode through the arched doorway behind the rose-entwined loggia and took her up the short twisting stairs beyond it. She blinked at the unexpected sight of a beautiful turreted room. Filmy draperies festooned a four-poster bed that had a fairytale presence which was enhanced by the gothic windows.

'Wow…' Katie felt rather as though she was in a dream from which she did not want to wake up.

'I know what you like,' Alexandros declared with roughened assurance, laying her down on the bed with an exquisite care that made her shiver with anticipation. 'I know exactly what you like.'

'Yes…' In the course of a split second her memory, unleashed from all self-discipline, doubled back eighteen months, to recall some of the wildly romantic things Alexandros had once done for her. Candles all round the bath and real rose petals floating on the surface of the water. Little unexpected gifts of perfume and cards and flowers. There had been a copy of a favourite book bound in leather, and a recording of a film she had not seen since childhood, which she had marvelled that he had found for her. He had seemed to have an astonishing understanding of what would make her happy. Her recollection began to move towards the tough conclusion of their affair, which had come as such a shock she had never really got over it, but she shut down and suppressed that dangerous slide back into the past.

'Katie…' Alexandros lowered his proud dark head to extract an exceedingly passionate kiss, and her hold on the past evaporated like a scary shadow she was afraid to acknowledge. 'I want you…'

When she looked up at his lean dark face, fierce longing flooded her, leaving no room for rational thought. Every inch of her felt tight, tense, restive. He ran his hands up over her breasts, grazing the prominent rosy tips in a skilful caress, and her back arched as the pleasure thrummed through her in an unstoppable tide. He bent his head there, and used his mouth to toy with the tender crests while he disposed of her last remaining garment.

As he parted her thighs she could feel herself melt deep down inside, and the level of her longing surged afresh. He traced the warm damp flesh at her feminine core, and the first quivering shock of delight claimed her passion-starved body. Abandoning herself to sensation, she was all slick wet heat and desire. He worked his skilful passage down over her writhing body, and before she could even guess what he intended, he subjected her to an intimacy that shocked her. His attentions were an exquisite torture. She went out of control as never before, with breathy little cries and shaken whimpers dragged from her parted lips. The feverish knot of hunger inside her tightened and tightened, until she reached an impossible height of craving and then went spinning wildly off into wave on wave of ecstatic release.

'Good…?'

Struggling for breath, Katie floated back to Planet Earth again, shattered at the intensity of what she had just experienced. She surveyed him with stunned eyes. 'More than…'

An unholy grin of satisfaction slashed his strong, sensual mouth. 'Good. I didn't give you the chance to surrender to your inhibitions…'

In a lithe movement, he settled between her slender thighs, his hands firm on her hips as he pushed her back and moved over her. She was full of languor, her body boneless and wondrously sensitised. He drove into her with a slow deep force that made her gasp and awakened her hunger again. Her lethargy vanished as he filled her to the hilt with the hot hard glide of his flesh, and the first jolt of renewed excitement rocked her.

'Please…' she whispered tightly, the inner rise of need gathering into pleasure-pain.

Alexandros gripped her hands in his and spread them wide, dominating her with his raw energy and passion. 'You feel so good,' he confided with ragged satisfaction, and a shade of disconcertion in his gaze. 'And I feel amazing…'

Her body had a life of its own, arching up in answer to his, while the wild excitement rose and rose until she reached yet another peak and lost herself in the drowningly sweet spasms of pleasure.

In the aftermath she was relaxed, so out of touch with reality that she felt as though she was floating in another world. The dizzy joy of release had spilled over into a fierce surge of emotion. She wrapped her arms round him and strung a drowsy line of kisses across his shoulder.

A husky laugh of appreciation vibrated through his lean hard frame, and he responded by tightening his hold on her slim body. 'I've missed you…you're so affectionate, *pedhi mou*.'

'I'm so sleepy,' she mumbled.

Alexandros eased her back against him and smoothed her tumbled hair back from her brow in a soothing motion. 'Then sleep.'

'Hmmm…' she muttered some timeless period later, when her body, languorous from slumber, was gently wakened to the erotic warmth and insistence of his. Every sense humming with response, she whispered his name in instant acceptance.

It was the most piercingly sweet experience of her life. A slow, deeply sensual joining of extreme pleasure that went on and on, until once again the ripples of release took hold of her. A powerful surge of profound joy and fulfilment washed over her. In that moment, with every defence lowered, words of love formed on her lips—and might have been spoken had not some sixth sense pulled her back from that dangerous brink and silenced her. It was the cruellest recall to the real world that she could have suffered.

'That was sublime, *pedhi mou*…' Alexandros told her lazily.

Her eyes opened, blank with shock and fear, a dark sense of *déjà-vu* tormenting her. She had slept with him again, fallen asleep in his arms like a trusting fool, and very nearly told him she loved him a second time. There, deep down inside her, below all the anger and the defensiveness, was the love she had thought she had overcome. Panic and confusion at the feelings she had concealed even from herself were swiftly followed by a flood of angry shame. This was the guy who had dumped her without regret. Had he really missed her? Yeah—so much so that he had never got in touch again! What had happened to that new beginning and the friendship he had suggested? Had he deliberately lulled her into a false sense of security? Those stray thoughts sparked more, one after the other.

Through wide, questioning eyes Katie stole a glance at the room. The décor was very feminine, a perfect match to her personal preferences, she conceded, with a frown starting to build between her feathery brows. Not only were pastels her favourite colours, but she also adored fresh flowers. Had she ever seen more roses and lilies gathered more prettily and less naturally in one place? What did it take to rouse her suspicions and put her on her guard? A fire alarm? A full-frontal attack with a military tank?

The picnic scenario had been equally calculated to provide special appeal, she reflected tautly. Cue for the exclusive magazine-spread approach to outdoor dining? A faint chill formed in her tummy and began to grow. She studied the beribboned silk knots embellishing the bedpost nearest her and almost choked on the conviction that it was all brand-new, that in fact she had been hooked like a fish by an expert angler. And, worse still, how many hours was it since she had seen or thought about her children? The lash of guilt that reflection induced was horrendous.

'You're very quiet.' Alexandros sighed. 'I hate to surrender our idyll, but I haven't eaten since breakfast, and it's now time for dinner.'

Thrusting herself away from him in an abrupt movement, Katie sat up. 'You've made a real fool of me...'

Lazily engaged in admiring the elfin quality her fragile features possessed, even with her hair all tousled and her make-up kissed off, Alexandros tensed and came up on one elbow to say, 'I don't think I quite follow.'

Katie leapt out of the bed as though she had had a sharp pin stuck into her shrinking flesh. The sun was sinking, but there was still more daylight than her modesty could stand coming through the tower windows. Nudity had never felt more damning or humiliating to her. Espying her panties on the rug, she swooped on them with shaking hands and clumsily climbed back into them.

Alexandros thrust back the tumbled sheet and sprang upright, a vision of lithe, bronzed masculinity. 'What's wrong?'

'I can't believe you can ask that question!' Katie raged. 'I made it so easy too, didn't I? Just give me a bit of sunlight, a cartload of roses and beautiful surroundings, and I fall for the whole seduction routine—'

'What seduction routine?' Alexandros hauled on his boxers and reached for his well-cut trousers. 'I have never had to seduce a woman in my life.'

'Don't you think for one moment that I will *ever* forget you doing this to me!' Katie launched at him, wrenching the sheet violently off the mattress and wrapping it round her in a series of jerky defensive movements. What remained of her underwear and her dress were still lying outdoors. Her cringing embarrassment felt like a fitting punishment for such wanton behaviour.

With tears of pain and anger burning the back of her green eyes, Katie raced down the spiral staircase. The incredible charm of the creased quilts, tumbled cushions and abandoned wine glasses in the beautiful leafy glade struck her afresh. She went rooting around for her bra and failed to find it.

'Have you gone crazy?' Alexandros enquired from the terrace, where he stood pulling on his shirt. 'One minute we're making love, the next you're screaming at me?'

'What happened to friendship?' she bawled at him.

Alexandros stilled, his shirt hanging loose and unbuttoned. Evening stubble made a sexy blue shadow round his wide, beautifully moulded mouth. Slumberous golden eyes full of immense power rested on her levelly. 'The option was there...you didn't go for it.'

Trembling with disbelief at that calm response, Katie stared back at him.

Alexandros extended a lean brown hand. 'Come back to bed, *thespinis mou*. I'll order food.'

She snatched up her dress, carefully unwound the sheet, and fought her way back into the garment in furious haste. 'You've just got to be joking! I came to Italy because I trusted you. Because I wanted to be fair to you and the children.'

Alexandros lifted expansive arms in a very Greek gesture and dropped them again. 'And you *have* been—for which I honour you. Today we moved on from the past...an important step—'

'The only place I moved on to was your bed, and I regard that as very much a retrograde step!'

'But you had a good time there,' Alexandros countered without hesitation. 'I heard no complaints.'

'That's not the point—'

Alexandros slung her a hard, shimmering smile that tensed her tummy muscles with a mixture of resentment and nerves. 'Perhaps your point is too illogical for me to follow. You wanted me.'

Furious tears in her eyes, Katie bent to lift and shake a quilt to locate her missing shoes. 'So it was okay to set me up, then, was it? Because I still find you attractive, you thought it would be fun to lure me out here with false talk of friendship?'

Watching her dig her dainty feet into her tiny shoes, Alexandros realised how much he liked that physical delicacy of hers. He groaned with impatience. 'I assure you that I am not finding this ridiculous scene fun. I still don't understand what the problem is.'

'Is that a fact?' Katie shot him a gleaming green glance full of bitterness. 'You don't see anything wrong with what you did?'

Lean, powerful face unyielding, Alexandros shrugged, a battle-hardened veteran when it came to avoiding direct and damning questions. 'What did I do?'

'Something that should've been beneath your precious honour after what you've already done to me. I should've smelt a rat the minute I saw this gorgeous picnic scene. It was too good to be true.'

Increasing frustration was starting to rise inside Alexandros. He was a very practical man. She liked fairy stories, floaty things, four-posters and flowers. He had ensured she got the lot and she *had* been enchanted. As far as he was concerned, everything had gone fantastically well: she'd been happy; he'd been happy. What was her problem? She was the only woman in his life who had ever shouted at him.

'Since when was giving you what you like and enjoy an *offence*?'

'It was all a sham—a nasty, manipulative, cheating sham.'

'*Theos mou*…I want to marry you!' Alexandros growled with incredulity. 'How was it a sham?'

Katie was so upset that it was a relief to espy her missing bra in the grass and have the excuse to stoop down to reclaim it. She closed a shaking hand over the small cotton garment. She hurt so much she wanted to scream. Because she knew she had wanted it all to be real, had wanted it so badly that she could still taste it.

'I asked you to marry me and you said no. I don't quit when I want something.' Alexandros dealt her a challenging look. 'That's who I am. That's what I'm about. I employed no deception.'

Outraged by his refusal to acknowledge fault, Katie straightened to her full height. 'Didn't you? You did all that romantic stuff for me before and it meant nothing! You encouraged me to care about you and then ditched me,' she condemned between clenched teeth, filled with hurt and mortification. Terrified that she would break down, she started back down the path through the woodland. 'Well, I'm not going to fall for the same empty charade again. You can't manipulate me like some business deal.'

'Define "romantic stuff".'

'The rose petals in the bath…the flowers…the cards… my favourite film…book,' she recited fiercely over one slight shoulder, enraged by his obtuseness.

Alexandros looked grim. 'I see no reason why so much significance should be awarded to several thoughtful treats and gifts,' he confided curtly. 'There was no intent to encourage or mislead you. I had not been in a relationship of that type before—'

'Yeah…I know. Is that why you referred to me as "just the maid" when you friend flew in for a visit?' Katie squeezed out a humourless laugh as she stalked back through the archway and down the cobbled lane.

Alexandros winced. She had overheard that?

'The friend was a gossip. I was protecting our privacy.'

Katie grimaced through the tears threatening her. 'No, you were telling the truth. That's all I ever was, all I was ever meant to be…the maid warming your bed.'

'You make it sound cheap and sordid, but it wasn't!' Alexandros thundered at her. 'The first day I allowed you to shout at me without fear of retribution you were no longer the maid. You were my equal!'

Taken aback by that explosion of temper, Katie shot him a startled glance and walked on faster than ever. 'Well, today was cheap… What did you do? Bring in decorators and stylists to set the scene for my seduction?'

'*Theos mou…*' Alexandros grated. 'As long as I live I will never try to please you again…you are the most contrary woman!'

'I don't trust you as far as I could throw you. Do you blame me?' Catching sight of the vast villa ahead, Katie spun round, hands planted on her slim hips to confront him again. 'Where were your security guards this afternoon? Their absence is proof that you planned to get me into bed!'

Alexandros spread lean brown hands in a graceful gesture. 'No comment…'

His obvious lack of shame outraged Katie to the brink of screaming. 'May you rot in hell for this, Alexandros Christakis!'

'It's not a crime for me to want to marry you—'

'Look, when I'm so desperate for a husband that I have to take one who just feels guilty that he got me pregnant, I'll let you know!'

Below the pillared portico of the giant villa, Alexandros brought her to a halt by the simple method of closing a lean brown hand over hers and holding fast until she was forced to turn back to him. 'Maybe I appreciate the existence of those

little boys much more than you give me credit for,' he bit out
in a raw undertone. 'Ianthe pursued every fertility treatment
known to the human race and still failed to conceive!'

Dumbfounded by that information, Katie stared at him
with wide, unblinking green eyes. Hurt and regret twisted
through her, and only caused more pain. Her very first
thought was that her own fertility must have struck him as
a bitterly ironic blow when his late wife had had to endure
repeated disappointment in her desire to bear his child.

'And maybe I'm also aware of how much I owe to my
grandparents for taking me into their home and raising me
as their son,' Alexandros completed.

'If I ever marry, I want a more personal connection with
my husband than my children,' she told him stiltedly.

As Katie spun on her heel and hurried into the villa,
Alexandros felt as if a detonator was going off inside him,
and he strode through the inner doors to the marble hall like
a tornado blowing in. 'What could be more *personal* than
what we have now?' he roared in her wake.

Astonished by his dark fury, scorched by the blaze of
his fierce golden stare, Katie stilled. 'That's just physical,'
she mumbled, in a tight dismissive tone.

'And what's wrong with that?' Alexandros grated in a
tone of naked aggression. 'I'd fly round the globe just to
spend one hour in your bed! It's the best sex I've ever had.
I'm happy with that—more than happy. Why can't you be?'

A floodtide of embarrassed colour flushed her face.
She could not initially credit that he had said that to her.
'Alexandros…'

Somewhere behind her she heard a cough. It sounded
very much like the sort of warning cough people employed
when they were keen to draw attention to their presence.
Before her very eyes Alexandros froze, his lean, darkly

handsome face shuttering, his lush lashes semi-screening his stunning eyes to wary glimmers of piercing gold.

'Alexandros…'

Slowly, reluctantly, her face very pink at the awareness that someone might have overheard a line or two of that ferocious and very private argument, Katie spun round. A white-haired older man, with her eldest son, Toby, comfortably clutched in one arm, was smiling widely at them both from the foot of the long hall.

'Pelias Christakis,' the old man acknowledged, in the most cheerful, friendly way. 'And you have to be—'

'Katie,' Alexandros sliced in flatly, closing his hand briefly over hers to palm the bra she held and dispose of it she knew not where—for his hand was empty when she dared to glance down again. 'Allow me to introduce you to my grandfather.'

Banding his free arm round Katie's taut spine, Pelias urged her to precede him into the drawing room. 'Katie…this is my wife—Calliope.'

A plump older lady, with shining silver hair and Connor cosily ensconced on her lap, greeted her in accented English.

Alexandros dismissed the nanny hovering in attendance while Katie felt that she was doing well not to succumb to an attack of hysterics. Her cheeks were certainly hot enough to fry eggs on. How long had Alexandros's grandparents been waiting for them to put in an appearance? Did they suspect the cause of their absence? They could hardly fail to have noticed that her hair was a tangled mop and her mascara smudged, and that Alexandros, mysteriously shorn of his usual sartorial elegance, lacked a jacket and socks. Nor could Pelias and Calliope have missed out on the fact that their grandson and the mother of their great-grandchildren had just been engaged in a ghastly argument. But neither of Alexandros's wonderfully charming grandparents betrayed the slightest hint of discomfort or disapproval.

Pelias beamed when Toby held out his arms to be reunited with Katie, and passed him back. 'Of course he wants his mother. Calliope and I were very excited when we heard about the children. I hope you will understand that we could not wait one day longer to meet them. Time is precious at our stage in life.'

Alexandros, who realised that he had been very wrong to assume that his grandparents were devastated by the scandal of his illegitimate sons, gritted his even white teeth. To his jaundiced gaze, the older couple looked as if all their Christmases had rolled in at once. He bent down to press a kiss to his grandmother's soft powdered cheek.

'Your grandfather wanted to warn you of our intended visit, but you know how much I love surprises,' she informed him chirpily.

'It's a wonderful surprise,' Alexandros responded without hesitation.

Explaining that arthritis made her a little stiff, Calliope invited Katie to come and sit beside her.

'They are wonderful little boys. Strong, healthy, full of life. You must be very proud of them,' Calliope remarked, petting Connor, who was lying back and enjoying every minute of such keen attention.

Equally misty-eyed, Pelias patted Toby's black curls before Katie lowered her son to the rug so that he could crawl. 'We are overjoyed by their existence.' He gave Katie a level look. 'I want you to know that, no matter what happens between you and Alexandros, we will always consider you and the children as a part of our family and you will be welcome in our home.'

Katie was touched to the heart by that sweeping declaration. She watched Toby making a beeline for his father.
The best sex I've ever had. Her face heating at the inop-
portune recollection, she was wildly aware of the ache
between her thighs. Their renewed intimacy had taken
her by storm—to such an extent that even meeting
Alexandros's eyes was a challenge.

'You'll stay for a few days, of course?' Alexandros was
saying quietly to his grandparents. 'Unfortunately I have
an early meeting in Brussels tomorrow, and will have to
leave later this evening. But Katie would welcome your
company.'

Extreme guilt assailed Katie. Was he making work an
excuse because of the row they had had? She watched
him scoop up Toby with an easy confidence that she
could see surprised and impressed the older couple.
Doubt and confusion engulfed her. The twins were
already learning to love their father. Had she made the
right decision? Or the wrong one? All her emotions were
at sixes and sevens; all her reactions seemed to be on a
razor's edge.

Half an hour later, Alexandros insisted on helping Katie
take the twins upstairs. Once they had been settled for the
night—the little boys had already eaten and been bathed—
he strolled back down the corridor with her and came to a
halt outside the bedroom that was to be hers for the duration
of her stay. 'I have one question I've been meaning to ask
you…it dates back to when you were carrying the twins.'

Katie glanced at him in surprise.

'When exactly did you make those calls to that phone
number I left with you?'

Katie compressed her generous pink mouth. 'It was the
summer…late June into July.'

Alexandros surveyed her with arrested dark golden eyes. 'And the letter you mentioned? When was it sent?'

'About the same time.'

'But that would have been six or seven months after we broke up. By then you must have known you were pregnant for a long time. Why did you wait until then before trying to contact me?' he demanded incredulously.

Katie almost winced, for it was a question she had hoped he would never ask. But now that he *had* asked she felt she had to give him an honest reply. 'I was waiting to see if you would phone me first.'

His ebony brows pleated. 'I don't get it.'

Katie lifted her chin, denying the raw sense of rejection she still felt. 'I wanted to know if you would get in touch with me again off your own bat. You didn't, which told me all I needed to know.'

'I'd have phoned if I'd known you were pregnant!' Alexandros launched back at her in disbelieving frustration. 'By the time you made the effort to call me, your name had been removed from the list—and that's why you didn't get to speak to me!'

'Some of us don't operate a datelined filing cabinet approach to our love-lives,' Katie murmured sourly.

At that crack, which was full of a defiant feminine logic utterly at war with the unemotional reserve, practicality and self-discipline that Alexandros prized, he drew in a slow, steadying breath of restraint. He was shocked to appreciate that he was a hair's breadth from losing his temper with her again. His scorching golden eyes veiled and cooled. Not with his grandparents still under the same roof. He had witnessed his grandfather's dismay that his grandson should even have raised his voice in Katie's vicinity. He had been dourly relieved that the older man's hearing loss would have prevented him from distinguishing words at such a distance. Unhappily, Pelias thought all women were like his wife—fragile flowers, with eternal smiles, adoring yielding natures and no temper whatsoever.

The only place Katie yielded was bed, Alexandros reflected grimly, reckoning that it was a great shame that he had ever allowed her out of the tower. Never again would he put food before sex. It was a time to think out of the box and come up with a fresh creative approach. But in the short term he felt he should step back and let her work out for herself what she was missing.

'Stay on here at the villa for a while,' Alexandros advised Katie equably, rising magnificently above that last comment of hers. 'It'll give me more time to sort out a suitable apartment for you in London.'

Katie was disconcerted at that change of subject, and at the calm agreement that she should have a home of her own. She looked up at him uncertainly. 'Alexandros…I understand if you're still annoyed with me, but I really feel we've taken a wrong turn and—'

'A couple of hours ago you were in my bed…don't please ask me to be friends now,' Alexandros incised with slashing derision. 'It's too late for that.'

'Maybe that was never a possibility,' Katie conceded, responding to a barely understood desire to soothe and placate that embarrassed her. She found it easy to argue with him, but the instant he started to pull back from her something perilously like panic took hold of her.

'Don't expect me to stand by and watch you bedding other men either.' Alexandros was determined to spell out her boundaries before he departed.

Dismayed that he could think that she would lurch straight out of his arms into another man's, Katie reached down to touch a lean brown hand in an intimate gesture that she did not even think about. 'I'm not like that. Don't you know that yet? I'm not planning—'

'You are pushing your luck.' Hard golden eyes glittering with warning, Alexandros backed her up against the wall and braced his hands on either side of her head, effectively imprisoning her. 'Don't touch if you don't want to be touched back, *pedhi mou.*'

Her breath snarled up in her throat and her mouth ran dry. The fire in his gaze set up a shameful tingle in her body. He was so close that she shivered, and she was shamed by the awareness that it was not apprehension that powered her. A helpless anticipation was making her heart-rate pick up speed

'You need to work on your resistance level, because I haven't given up,' Alexandros spelt out, soft and low like a purring tiger. 'When I want something, I go all out to get it. The next round, I may well fight dirty, *thespinis mou.*'

With a sardonic smile, he dropped his hands, straightened, and stepped back with exaggerated courtesy to allow her free passage.

CHAPTER SEVEN

FOUR weeks later, Katie attended the opening of an art gallery in the company of a handsome young Greek businessman and his sister.

When she had returned from Italy Alexandros had been in New York, and she had spent more than a week as a guest in Pelias and Calliope Christakis's comfortable London home. There she had met a lot of people, because the sociable older couple had made a special effort to draw her into their social circle. Damon and Eugena Bourikas, who had initially visited Pelias and Calliope in the company of their elderly father, had been welcome new acquaintances as they were in Katie's own age group.

For the first time in a long time Katie was in a position to enjoy a social life, and she was trying to push herself out and about to do exactly that. She was also planning to look for a part-time office job, to ease her back into the swing of working life. The breathtaking speed of change over the past weeks, however, had challenged her more than she had expected.

She had finally picked up the courage to phone her mother in New Zealand and tell her about the twins. The news that she was a grandmother had come as a shock to

Maura. Although she had been hurt that her daughter had
not confided in her, she had phoned Katie back a day later
to ask a flood of questions about the little boys and request
some photos of them.

Although Katie was now free of any immediate financial or accommodation woes, she was suffering from
shamefully low spirits—which she did her best to conceal
behind a cheerful smile. She felt that a job would give her
a fresh focus. If she got back into the employment market
she would start earning some independence again. Was
she planning to live as some sort of kept woman on
Christakis largesse for ever? No way. And perhaps a return
to the workplace would give her something better to think
about than the fact that she missed seeing Alexandros.
That intense sting of loss wasn't getting any easier to bear
with the passage of time. He had been abroad a great deal
on business. He had also contrived to visit the twins on
three separate occasions when she was out; what contact
they *had* enjoyed had been bereft of privacy and distinctly
edgy in tone.

Only a week had passed since Katie had moved in to the
stunning fully furnished apartment which Alexandros had
organised for her. It was infinitely larger, fancier and more
centrally located than she could ever have envisaged.
Alexandros, however, had dismissed her protests with the
declaration that his sons had a right to benefit from every
possible advantage and comfort.

'I guess the rumours about you and Alexandros
Christakis must be true.' Damon Bourikas allowed that
provocative statement to trail in the air while they
wandered round the gallery exhibits.

Wishing his sister had not drifted off, leaving them
alone, Katie tensed. 'I never talk about Alexandros…'

'Did the tabloids say it all for you?' the young Greek riposted.

Katie went scarlet. 'My goodness, that was *all* rubbish! What are the rumours you mentioned?'

'That you're not together in any way with him. I made the comment because I saw your nanny when she brought the children to visit Pelias and Calliope.'

Katie studied him in bewilderment. 'I don't understand…'

'Your nanny, Maribel, is a seriously tasty package,' Damon explained. 'Only a woman unafraid of competition would employ a nanny who resembles a supermodel in her home. Particularly one who is an exact match of the female profile preferred by the Christakis males: a leggy blonde with heavenly curves…'

As his meaning sank in, Katie turned bone-white. Until that moment Katie had never thought about the fact that Maribel was a beauty, but now her thoughts went into overdrive. Did the nanny's undeniable charms explain Alexandros's recent visits to the twins when she herself was elsewhere and unavailable? Was Damon trying to give her a warning? Was Alexandros chasing her nanny and was she, Katie, the very last to know?

'Yes, she is lovely, isn't she?' Katie managed to say through teeth that were almost chattering from the sudden chill that was creeping through her taut body. 'I suppose she might remind him of his late wife.'

'She would be a hard act to follow, I would think.'

'Who are you talking about?' His sister Eugena, a talkative brunette, rejoined them at that point.

'Ianthe Christakis,' Damon supplied.

'My mother used to hold her up to me as a role model,' Eugena confided with a rueful expression. 'Of course Ianthe was much older than me. She was gorgeous, though, and always doing charity work. She was also totally devoted to Alexandros—'

'He married her and turned into a workaholic,' Damon remarked.

'Everybody knows that they had the perfect marriage!' Eugena shot her brother a look of reproof.

Thrown off-balance by Eugena's generous litany of praise, Katie swallowed hard. 'Pelias and Calliope never mention Ianthe.'

'They were all devastated when she died. It was so tragic that she never had a child.' Then, as if realising what she was saying, Eugena reddened with discomfiture. 'I'm sorry, Katie. I hope you don't think I meant—'

'No, of course not.' Katie smiled with all her might, but there was a hollow sensation inside her.

Well, she had asked and she had been told, she thought numbly, wandering round the exhibits in Damon and Eugena's wake and scarcely knowing what she said when pressed for an opinion on the various works of art. All Katie could think about was that Ianthe had been a genuinely wonderful wife, and Alexandros had been very happy with her. For the first time Katie was forced to confront the demon of her own jealousy. She was desperately ashamed of those feelings, but she still could not shake free of them. She was horribly jealous of what Alexandros had had with Ianthe, and knowing that she had no right to feel that way made little difference. Even so, she was disturbed by the awareness that bitter jealousy and injured pride had prevented her from giving serious consideration to his marriage proposal. On the other hand, was she really so desperate that she had to consider marrying a guy who had openly said that sex was all she had to offer him?

Alexandros had loved his wife. He had been grieving for

Ianthe when he'd met Katie, and he had used Katie like a sticking plaster on the wound—easily discarded once he was on the road to recovery. In comparison to Ianthe she had been a casual fling, a temporary deviation from his sophisticated norm, and only the birth of Toby and Connor had given Katie a passport back into Alexandros's life. She saw that those painful truths had savaged her self-esteem and made her deny the fact that she was still hopelessly in love with the twins' father. But she also saw that she really did need to get over her less than presentable emotions about his late wife and his perfect marriage. The very fact that Alexandros regarded the subject of Ianthe as too private and personal ever to be discussed only reminded Katie that she was still very much on the outside looking in.

When the gallery opening was drawing to a close, Katie faked a yawn and turned down an invite to travel on to a party. Damon offered to take her home.

'There's a car waiting for me…'

Damon raised a brow. 'I'll see you out. So, you're not free after all?'

'I don't know what you mean.'

'Your children aren't here, but you're still running about in a chauffeur-driven limo. It's an ownership statement. Christakis is posting very large "Keep off the Grass" signs all round you,' the young Greek quipped.

'Not necessarily,' Katie muttered uncomfortably as they emerged onto the dark street. 'I usually take the boys everywhere with me, and Alexandros insists that I use the car.'

'Anyway, don't worry about your nanny's fatal attraction,' Damon told her smugly. 'If she's available, I intend to keep her fully occupied!'

As that expression of interest in Maribel sank in, a flash of light from a camera almost blinded Katie, and she blinked in surprise like a myopic owl. The photographer sped off, and Damon urged her into the limo. 'I'm surprised Christakis didn't give you a bodyguard as well.'

'He did… I told him I didn't need him tonight,' Katie sighed.

After a night spent pretty much tossing and turning, she got up to feed and dress Toby and Connor the next morning and went back to bed when Maribel arrived. It felt like only five minutes later when an urgent knock woke her again, and the door opened a crack.

'Mr Christakis is here, asking for you…'

Katie threw herself out of bed, glanced in the mirror, and almost loosed a shriek of anguish. Her hair was an explosive tangle of ringlets. Why did he have to come calling on her without warning at this unearthly hour of the day? A belated glance at the alarm clock informed her that it was actually mid-morning, for she had slept longer than she'd appreciated. In a frantic rush, she cleaned her teeth, splashed her face and hurriedly pulled on some clothes, emerging from her room breathless, to hurry into the sitting room.

But Alexandros wasn't there. He was in the nursery, with the twins and Maribel. Katie hovered unnoticed in the doorway, finger-combing her copper ringlets to make them flatter and smoothing down her black T-shirt and denim skirt. She wished she had taken the time to put on make-up and shoes. Alexandros was asking questions and Maribel was answering, her pink-cheeked smiles and flickering upward glances the response of a susceptible woman in the presence of a very fanciable and smoulderingly sexy guy.

'Alexandros…'

He swung round and focussed incisive golden eyes on her. There was no smile on his lean, extravagantly handsome face. As he accompanied her to the sitting room, she found herself wondering if her interruption had been an unwelcome one.

'Do you find Maribel attractive?' Suddenly what Katie was worrying about, what she was trying not to think about, spilled from her lips in an unstoppable rush.

The most ghastly silence fell. It seemed to eddy out round her, as if she was trapped in the centre of a whirlpool. In the long stretch of quiet that followed she did feel as if she was drowning, as intense mortification crawled through her. Nothing would have persuaded her to look at him.

'Let me get this straight…' Alexandros was framing English words with the greatest difficulty because he was outraged by the question. 'You're asking me if I want to shag the nanny?'

Hot colour spread across her cheeks. 'That's not what I meant—'

'Of course it is. The answer is no. I don't ever hit on my staff, and I sack them if they try it on with me. You're the single exception—the only employee who has ever ended up in my bed—'

'And taking the fallout of that into consideration, I'm sure it's not a risk you'd choose to take again.'

Alexandros surveyed her with brooding force. With the sexual pull she exerted over him, he was wondering what choice had to do with it. He hadn't liked the way she made him feel then, and he really liked it little better now. But he knew that given the same situation he would repeat the exact same behaviour pattern. In the outfit she was wearing, with her little pink unpainted toes curling into the rug, she looked absurdly young and naive—until she glanced up from below those feathery lashes with witch-green irides-cent eyes that had the most sinful effect on his libido.

'You were with Damon Bourikas last night…explain,'

Alexandros invited coolly, the lust on his mind steadily spreading to even more responsive areas.

Her head came up, chin angling. 'Excuse me…?'

'He's not fit company for you.'

'I'm an adult. I can't believe you're saying that to me—'

'I don't want you associating with him.'

'Nobody tells me who I socialise with—'

Disturbingly calm golden eyes assailed hers. 'I do…and if you don't listen Bourikas certainly will. Because I'm too influential for him to ignore.'

'You wouldn't dare,' Katie told him shakily, her temper sparking with incredulity at that threat.

'Oh, I think we both know that I would, and with pleasure, *yineka mou*,' Alexandros responded with provocative silkiness. He had been incensed when he saw that photo in the morning paper. Damon bloody Bourikas! Rumour linked Bourikas to some very wild parties—but Alexandros had no intention of telling Katie that, in case a bad-boy image increased Damon's sleazy appeal. He was already grimly conscious that, at barely twenty-five years old, the other man was much closer to her age than he was.

Of course the sensible thing to do would be to tell Alexandros that Damon was interested in their gorgeous French nanny, Katie reflected grudgingly. But her pride revolted against that course. And if Alexandros should think that another man was interested in her, it might make her seem more exciting and desirable in his eyes. Alexandros was very competitive in business. Mightn't he prove equally competitive when it came to a woman? It was not the moment to tell him that Damon was too flash and smugly assured of his own charms to attract her.

'You seem to be forgetting that I met Damon in your grandparents' home,' she reminded him.

'They keep an open house. You are not in a position to be careless of appearances,' Alexandros delivered.

Katie breathed in so deep she was afraid that her lungs would burst. Being told that by the guy responsible for turning her into an unmarried mother galled her. 'And why would that be?'

Brilliant dark golden eyes enhanced by inky black lashes rested on her. 'One Greek tycoon…?' He shifted a graceful lean brown hand in an accepting motion. 'But being seen around town with a *second* rich Greek could suggest that you're making a lucrative lifestyle choice.'

Katie went bright pink with bristling fury at that insult. 'How…dare…you?'

'I dare because your reputation matters to me, and to our children.'

Her hands knotted into fists, but that very first reference to the twins as something they shared did not pass her by. 'I make my friends where I choose!'

'No,' Alexandros murmured with lethal finality, strolling closer and taking her hands in his to slowly, intently, unwind her angrily knotted fingers and curl them into his own. 'You're not on your own any more.'

'Hands off! You're the one who warned me not to touch!' Katie reminded him breathlessly.

Lush black lashes screened his gaze to a sliver of gold as hot as sunlight on the animated triangle of her flushed and furious face. He could feel the passion vibrating in her tiny frame, and it drew him like a starving man to life-giving food. 'I like an element of risk. It adds an edge,' he murmured thickly.

The silence hummed with energy, and she snatched in a breath, holding her slight body very taut. But the stirring heaviness of her breasts and the little twist of heat at the heart of her were too pressing to ignore, and bewilderment flashed through her eyes. 'But we're having a fight…'

'I don't want to fight with you,' Alexandros imparted very softly, deciding then and there that when playing it cool sentenced him to celibacy, he had played it cool for long enough.

'I have to take Toby and Connor out for a walk,' she told him hurriedly, struggling to suppress and sidestep the physical awareness that was threatening her self-control.

Releasing her hands, Alexandros startled her by walking out to the hall. He reappeared barely a minute and a half later.

'What were you doing?' Katie almost whispered.

'I was telling your nanny that the boys need some fresh air.'

Katie blinked. 'But…but why did you do that? For goodness' sake, it makes it look as if—'

'It's not her job to think about how anything looks. You have such touchingly naive concerns, *pedhi mou*.' Stunning dark golden eyes rested on her with a measured power that fired colour into her fair skin. 'Come here…'

'No way…absolutely no way!' Katie asserted with feverish intensity.

Alexandros jerked loose his tie and, unbuttoning his jacket, shrugged his shoulders out of it and tossed it on an armchair.

Green eyes huge, Katie stared at him. 'What are you doing?'

'What does it look like I'm doing?'

His mobile phone buzzed like an angry wasp. He pulled out, gave it a regretful look, sighed, and switched it off without ceremony.

'But that's probably the bank and terribly important!' Katie protested, as he cast his tie alongside his jacket and her sense of panic and confusion rose to suffocating proportions.

'*Theos mou*…do you think I always do what people expect me to do? Sometimes obeying one's natural instincts feels more right than following the rules. This is one of those times.' Loosening his collar, he embarked on his shirt buttons.

'Stop!' Katie gasped, hot-faced.

'If I stop, I leave…and I start looking for someone else.' Brilliant dark golden eyes watched her absorb that statement and turn as ashen pale as though some vital life force was being leeched from her.

The very thought of Alexandros with another woman tore Katie to shreds. Just that one little mention of that option and she was living her worst nightmare. Dry-mouthed and trembling, Katie watched a bronzed segment of muscular torso appear between the parted edges of his fine cotton shirt. Her heart was beating very, very fast. 'You're threatening me—'

'No, I'm being brutally honest, *glikia mou*. Did you think I would wait for ever? Either you want me or you don't…'

'Getting married is—'

'No.' Alexandros spread lean brown hands. 'This is much more basic. I'm not talking about marriage. Leave that out of it. You don't know what you want, and it's time you did. I want to go to bed with you, but I don't want a four-act tragedy after it.'

Her chin tilted, green eyes sparkling, cheeks pink. 'I don't like the idea of you with someone else!' she flung back at him chokily, anger and pain coalescing in that forced admission.

Alexandros strolled closer. There was so much all-conquering hero in the blaze of primal satisfaction in his gaze that she was tempted to release her tension by slapping him for an opportunism that smacked of piracy. Furious tears glistening in her eyes, she hissed shakily, 'Sometimes I hate you so much I could scream!'

Alexandros tugged her to him with strong, determined hands. 'I know…and it's refreshing to be with a woman who occasionally finds fault with me,' he conceded, without a shade of irony.

Feeling like a feather fluttering up against a solid steel wall of assurance, she rested her brow against his chest. The rich, awesomely familiar scent of his skin assailed her and she trembled. She loved him; she hated herself. He had forced her into a tight corner and emerged triumphant with a truth she would never have willingly given him: all her proud independence and defiance was destroyed by the very thought of him slaking that high-voltage sex drive of his in the arms of another woman.

He smoothed her hair almost clumsily, and expelled his breath on a slow, measured hiss. 'A month is a long time for me…too many cold showers, endless lonely nights.'

Against her stomach she could feel the hard male heat of him, and her tummy flipped in response. Long fingers knotting in her ringlets, he claimed her generous pink lips with a voracious hunger that made her knees give way under her. Bundling her up into his arms with easy strength, he tumbled her down on the sofa and let his tongue delve with erotic precision into her mouth, while he eased her slender thighs apart to explore the taut stretch of fabric that concealed her most secret place from him. He stifled her helpless whimper of need with his lips when she jack-knifed beneath the tormenting stroke of his lean fingers, every sensual nerve jangling with urgency.

He pushed up her T-shirt, let his teeth graze a stiff pink crest, dallied there while she arched her hips and gasped, insanely conscious of his every move and her terrifying response. All sensation was centred at the damp hot core at the heart of her. He drew up her knees, tugged down her panties, and told her hungrily that lace-edged white cotton was a real turn-on. The tightness low in her pelvis made it impossible for her to stay still. She dug her hands into his shoulders and pulled him back to her, driven by a need so powerful it was a consuming instinct.

'Don't stop…' she pleaded frantically when he lifted his arrogant dark head.

Passionate dark golden eyes slammed into hers. 'We need to get a couple of things straight—'

'Not now!'

'No more nonsense about friendship,' Alexandros decreed raggedly, hauling her to the edge of the sofa with strong hands. 'No more references to duty or love. Let this be pure, perfect enjoyment for both of us.'

Katie wouldn't let herself think about what he was saying. Her body was on fire for him, singing a pagan song of shameless craving. She knew conscience was going to kill her, but she was prepared to pay the piper. He plunged into the hot satin heat of her receptive depths and she almost passed out with pleasure. What followed was the wildest, hottest excitement she had ever dreamt she might experience, and at the summit an incredibly intense climax.

Afterwards she clung to him, dimly wondering if she was in heaven, trying not to be shocked by the fact that they were both still wearing most of their clothes.

'I needed that,' Alexandros confessed hoarsely, seeking and demanding a passionate kiss that demonstrated a renewed hunger that took her aback. He laughed huskily when she looked up at him in bemusement. 'I really, really needed that, *pedhi mou*…and I need so much more.'

He lifted her up into his arms, clamped her legs round his waist, and carried her out of the room.

'No…what about—?'

'Our children were safely off the premises *before* you started screaming with pleasure.' Alexandros pressed his mouth hotly to the sensitive skin below her ear and began doing something so impossibly erotic she moaned out loud.

'I didn't scream,' she mumbled belatedly as he brought her down on her bed.

'You will this time.' With single-minded efficiency Alexandros was stripping off her T-shirt and her skirt, yanking the duvet out of her grasp before she could scramble out of sight below it. 'No…I'm a big boy. I get to look all I like.'

'Alexandros!' she wailed, jerking up to hug her knees. 'I can't—'

'Please…' he said, for the first time, burnished golden eyes smouldering over her.

'It would make me feel shameless—'

'Shameless in the bedroom works well for me.' Meeting her strained gaze, Alexandros hastened to add, 'But only if it's you…'

She shut her eyes tight and lowered her knees, lay down like a sacrifice on a slab.

'You can blush in places that I didn't know could blush,' Alexandros breathed not quite steadily, rearranging her slender body into a slightly more daring pose. 'But if you don't look back at me I'll feel like a voyeur…'

Katie went rigid, and then lifted her lashes.

'That's perfect.' Alexandros spoke very quietly, tugging her hands very gently back down to her sides when they made a sudden sneaking attempt to cover up her most interesting areas. 'You're so beautiful…'

She frowned. 'No, I'm not—'

'You are to me,' he told her truthfully, admiring her delicate porcelain-pale curves with immense appreciation, and only vaguely wondering why it was the most intensely erotic moment of his life.

'I'm really not.'

'There may not be much of you, but what you have is in great proportion. Your hair is an amazing colour, and though your nose may turn up like an elf's it suits your face. I like your eyes, and your mouth, a hell of a lot,' Alexandros breathed, pitching his shirt off and disposing of what remained of his clothing with a haste that was possibly more flattering than his honest appraisal of her looks.

'Anything else?' Katie was not too chuffed about the elf crack, but his enthusiasm was undeniable.

'You're so natural…' His slumberous gaze devoured her with earthy boldness. He drew her back to his hotly aroused length, curved long fingers to her pouting breast with distinct satisfaction. 'There's nothing false, nothing surgically enhanced. Half the time you don't even wear make-up.'

'Everything's so physical with you,' Katie muttered shakily.

'You'll get used to it, and learn to like it that way.' Alexandros tugged gently on a swollen pink nipple and wrenched a responsive gasp from her. She quivered like a vibrating piano wire against him. He smiled with approval and let his carnal mouth nuzzle the tender skin of her throat, while he continued to caress her wildly sensitive flesh.

'But there could be so much—'

'No…' Alexandros leant over her, all domineering male, reproof in every powerful line of his lean, gorgeous face. 'This time we do it my way. Simple, straight, nothing messy…'

Moisture prickled at the back of her eyes. She refused to believe that his relationship with Ianthe had been based on straightforward sex. He had loved his wife. He would never, ever love her in the same way. How many times did he have to spell that out to her? When she had told him she loved him in Ireland he had ditched her faster than the speed of light, because her confession had filled him with distaste.

Alexandros could feel her tensing, trying to impose some space between them, and he didn't like that. He kissed her and held her fast, employing every erotic skill in his considerable repertoire to keep her close.

He made love to her again, and then again, until she was so drowsy that she could hardly keep her eyes open. It was as if he couldn't get enough of her. In spite of the ache of hurt at the back of her mind, she couldn't help but be thrilled by the sheer strength of his desire.

She was half asleep when she realised that he was no longer beside her. Black hair still gleaming from the shower, Alexandros was fixing his silk tie and fully dressed.

'You're leaving?' she whispered in surprise.

'A rescheduled meeting to replace the one I skipped earlier. I have to be in Rome tomorrow, and I go from there to Hong Kong,' he admitted, watching her sexily tousled reflection in the mirror like a hawk.

Consternation filled Katie and she sat up, feeling horrendously forsaken and forlorn. 'When will you be back?'

Alexandros breathed in deep, questioning why her obvious disquiet at his departure from the country should act on him like a shot of adrenalin. She didn't want him to leave and she couldn't hide it. Clingy, needy behaviour usually repelled him, left him cold as ice. But when Katie looked stricken at the prospect of having to get by without him it lit a blazing fire of burning satisfaction inside him.

In fact it made him feel happy. He wondered why that was, then acknowledged how fortunate it was for the stability of their children that he *did* feel that way.

Not an atom of that rare instance of self-examination showed on his lean, bronzed face. 'I'm not sure. I'll call…'

Katie nodded like a marionette.

'Doesn't this feel good?' Alexandros gave her a brilliant bracing smile, mentally willing her to follow his lead and act more upbeat. 'No stress, no strain. This is how I always wanted it to be between us, *thespinis mou*.'

Katie listened to the thud of the front door on his exit. He was gone and the apartment was silent. Her throat thickened. *How he'd always wanted it to be:* loads of sex, without love, ties or demands. He was much happier than he had been when he was proposing marriage. And why was that? She had agreed to his terms and, without quite realising how it had come about, it registered that she appeared to have fallen into the role of his mistress. Her eyes watered. She willed the stupid tears back and strove to work out how the heck that had happened, and what on earth she was planning to do about it…

CHAPTER EIGHT

A RARE smile on his wide, passionate mouth, a laden gift box clutched below one powerful arm, Alexandros stepped into the lift in Katie's apartment block. Although he loathed surprises, he knew that she loved them—and he couldn't wait to see her face when she realised that he was back in London thirty-six hours sooner than he had forecast. He had worked impossibly long hours to manage that feat.

During his eight days abroad he had spent an entire evening shopping—and he hated shopping. He had enjoyed the toy stores, though, he conceded, wishing that Katie was as easy to please in the gift stakes as their sons. His level ebony brows pleating, he wondered tautly if he had got it right this time. It was ironic that he knew exactly what Katie liked. Long after he had parted from her he had often found himself seeing something and thinking that Katie would have loved it, whether it was a view, a piece of music, an item of clothing or a joke. He had no idea why he had always understood her tastes so well. Perhaps he listened better than most men, and he had a very retentive memory. Or perhaps it was down to the fact that he was highly observant. But when he had been with Katie in Ireland he had really enjoyed buying her presents, and watching a look of wonder and delight blossom in her hugely expressive eyes.

Before he'd met her, his staff had bought the gifts he gave to women, and they had always been very expensive and impersonal. This time around he had been very careful about what he bought for Katie. He had walked right past a half-dozen items that he had known she would adore. He had purchased no cute cards, no flowers, no favourite anythings that might risk giving her that fatal romantic message and lead to further accusations of deception. So he'd opted for Chantilly lace lingerie with a top designer label. After all, there was nothing wrong with selfishness. He was also hoping that the platinum and diamond pendant carrying the initial 'K' that he had bought from the world's most expensive jeweller would magically exorcise his current infuriating and spooky habit of doodling that same letter every time he got a pen in his hand.

Unlocking the door of the apartment with his key, he was surprised by the noisy thump of music, playing loud enough to shake the rafters. He hadn't realised that Katie was a rock fan, but he was pleased that she was evidently at home. He went straight into the sitting room. She wasn't there, but evidence in the shape of the empty bottle of champagne lying on its side suggested that she was entertaining. Where?

A garment lay on the limestone floor of the corridor that led to the rest of the apartment. His brows descending over frowning dark golden eyes, Alexandros bent and hooked a finger into the item. It was a man's purple shirt, and it was *not* one of his. In the same second he made that deduction, it was as if the entire world went into a crazy time-warp. He broke into a sweat, every muscle in his big powerful frame locking into rigidity. The incessant driving beat of the music seemed to swell like the roaring riptide of emotion surging through him. Through the door to the left he could hear a wailing sound that went beyond the level of the music. It was Toby and Connor, crying...

Although instinct urged him to check on them, his savage, glittering gaze was locked to the door ahead, which stood wide open on Katie's bedroom. He strode on to the threshold and saw the naked couple on the mattress. He recognised Damon Bourikas first, and he was about to haul him off the bed and kill him when he registered that the woman in Katie's bed was definitely not Katie. It was Maribel the nanny, an over-endowed blonde, engaged in an act that Katie was still not sophisticated enough to know about. Disgust and relief combined with such force inside Alexandros that he felt momentarily light-headed. When he hit the off button on the entertainment centre to silence the thundering rock chorus, he noticed the scattering of fine white powder and the rolled-up note on the dressing table. He went white with rage and repugnance.

'The party's over. Get out before I call my security team up to throw you out the way you are!'

Damon attempted to make a laughing apology in a flood of Greek.

Alexandros cut in to tell him that it if they weren't gone in minutes he would be calling the police. He strode into the nursery, where one glance at Toby and Connor's red and swollen faces was sufficient to tell him that his sons must have been crying for attention for a good deal longer than a few minutes. His hands clenched into furious fists. Shorn of their usual bouncy confidence, the babies looked pathetic, and pitifully grateful to see him. The sight of their helplessness kicked his heart wide open.

In truth he felt distinctly weird, he conceded, raking

long fingers through his cropped black hair and registering in astonishment that his hand was trembling. For some inexplicable reason he could not stop reliving that sick instant when he had actually believed that Katie might be in bed with another guy. Having sex with someone else, betraying him, cheating on him. Perspiration dampened his skin, and it was but a prelude to the startling rolling tide of nausea that took sudden hold of him. He made it into the *en suite* bathroom in the nick of time. *Theos mou*, what was the matter with him? He was never ill. Had he picked up an infection?

Only ten minutes ago he had been riding high, after a phenomenally successful trip and the awed approbation of all his staff. He had travelled straight from the airport to see Katie and the children. The whole sordid scene he had interrupted had outraged his every principle: drug abuse in a property he owned, a sleazeball like Bourikas daring to desecrate Katie's fluffy girlie bedroom, the nanny neglecting their children. But would that have made him physically sick? Made him feel as though a brick wall had suddenly fallen on him?

One of the twins sobbed, shooting him back out of his bemused introspection. Katie hadn't been in bed with anyone, he reminded himself with fierce exasperation. Later she would be very much in bed with *him*, in his bed at Dove Hall. That was not negotiable. He had been too patient. But now he would take charge of the situation the way he should have done from the start.

Having washed, he contemplated his sons. He was down a nanny. Where was Katie? He could phone her, or call in reinforcements. Or he could look after them himself for a while. He lifted the little boys out of their cots. They were damp and needed to be changed. When had they last eaten?

He thought about reinforcements again, but conscience won out: it would be cruel to let strangers handle them straight after what they had suffered. After removing his suit jacket, tie, and his diamond cufflinks, he found clean clothes for the twins and got down to work. Two hours later he called Cyrus to come and give him a hand to get the children down to the limo.

'Don't ask,' Alexandros warned his head of security when the older man was presented with Toby, clad only in a nappy and a chocolate-smeared blanket. His brother was in a similar state. But it was Alexandros who had fared worst of all: bathwater, chocolate stains, biscuit crumbs, spilt milk and juice had destroyed his usual elegance. His black hair sat up in little clumps where it had been clutched by sticky fingers.

When the children were secure in their car seats he took a deep breath and relaxed for the first time in two hours. He fell asleep. The limo was well on the way to Dove Hall before he lifted the phone to call the twins' mother.

'You're a kind girl.' Calliope Christakis gave Katie's hand an affectionate squeeze. 'I hope you get that job.'

'Even though Alexandros will go mad?' That morning Katie had had an interview for a receptionist's position with an upmarket property agency. After it she had met up with Calliope and accompanied the older woman to a dental appointment that she had been dreading. Lunch and a shopping trip had followed.

'A little of what he doesn't like does him good,' his grandmother told her cheerfully. 'Imagine him telling you that it is his *duty* to marry you! All that education and he says that. Of course you said no. He's a Christakis and a banker. He'll come up with a better offer.'

'We'll see…' Katie wished that she had managed to hold firm against Calliope's gentle interrogation technique of questions and seemingly casual comments. When Calliope had hinted that she thought less of her grandson for not offering Katie a more stable relationship, Katie had just had to speak up on Alexandros's behalf. Now, kissing his grandmother's cheek, she promised to come for lunch soon with Toby and Connor, and took her leave.

When Alexandros phoned her she was letting herself back into her apartment. Frowning, she murmured, 'What do you mean…the twins aren't here?'

In a few graphic sentences, Alexandros outlined the scene he had interrupted. Her heart sank like a stone. She was horrified, for she had been out all day. 'Maribel seemed so nice…' she mumbled in a daze.

'Sadly, that doesn't mean she was also a responsible person. With hindsight, perhaps she was too young.'

Having assured Katie that Toby and Connor were fine, Alexandros suggested that she pack whatever she and the children would require for a weekend at Dove Hall.

'Are you blaming me for this?' she whispered.

'No. But I won't let it happen again, *yineka mou*.'

While she packed, Katie wondered what he had meant by that closing comment. Hadn't *she* chosen Maribel for the job? As she was about to leave the apartment she found the bag he had discarded in the hall and unwrapped his gifts. Tears sparkled in her eyes as she attached the diamond pendant round her throat. She studied the lingerie with hot cheeks and stuffed it surreptitiously into her weekend bag, next to the toys he had bought for the boys.

Desperate to be reunited with her sons, Katie raced into the country house and straight up to the nursery. Toby and Connor were fast asleep in their cots, and she breathed again, feeling a little foolish for her concerns. Even so, she was painfully aware that something much more serious might have happened to her children.

Alexandros was in the library, on the phone. Lounging back against his desk, he indicated that she wait, and she wandered over to the huge windows that overlooked the lush green grassy slopes which ran all the way down to the edge of the classic lake. While Alexandros talked in Greek her eyes ate him up, in a series of avid stolen glances that were too nervous to linger.

He was so beautiful, she thought painfully. When he had been abroad she had told herself that she had gained control of her feelings for him. She had thought that her love was at a reasonable rather than obsessional level. And now one glimpse of him had exploded that foolish illusion. There he was, his classic bronzed profile silhouetted against the daylight, turning back towards her, black hair gleaming, inky spiky lashes long enough to cast a shadow on his superb high cheekbones, tawny eyes with that stunning golden impact. He still made her feel as giddy and breathless as a teenager.

'Toby and Connor look quite untouched by all the excitement,' she confided.

'That's not what you'd have said if you'd seen them when we arrived here,' Alexandros admitted wryly. 'I took care of them for a couple of hours at the apartment and I got them in a mess.'

'Why didn't you ring me? I would have come straight home.'

'For some reason I assumed you'd be back soon, and…I am their father.' Alexandros shrugged a broad shoulder. 'I thought I should be capable of looking after them on my own for an hour or so. Pride comes before a fall. I'm *not* capable.'

Katie was amazed and touched that he had even made the attempt. 'What happened?'

After the nightmare ordeal of bathing the twins, he had found it impossible to get clothes on to their squirming and uncooperative little bodies. When he had tried to feed them, everything he had offered had been rejected in favour of the chocolate biscuits he had been eating himself. Unable to get the biscuits back again, he had surrendered to the screams and thrown in the towel.

'At least you tried,' Katie pointed out bracingly, lifting a hand to touch the glittering pendant at her throat, her green eyes warm with appreciation. 'And I love this…it's beautiful. I wish I'd been at home when you arrived.'

Studying her, Alexandros savoured her pleasure and her appearance. He liked the way she was dressed. In a grey pencil skirt, teamed with a white slash-necked top, her feet adorned with strappy high heels, she looked enchantingly small and feminine and ravishingly pretty. He thought it a shame that he was about to spoil the ambience.

'Right now we have something more imperative to consider,' Alexandros drawled levelly. 'I have tried to deal with this relationship on your terms and it's not working.'

'You *are* blaming me! Don't you think I feel bad enough on my own account? You warned me about Damon and I didn't listen…and he had already told me that he was after Maribel—'

'You *knew* that? I thought that it was you he was interested in.'

Saving face on that score was no longer an option, Katie registered painfully, and she went pink with discomfiture. 'No.'

That small point cleared up, Alexandros looked grave. 'I'll be frank. I want my children living with me where there are adequate staff to ensure that what happened today never happens again.'

'But that's not possible,' Katie protested ruefully.

'It is if you marry me. And I'm not asking this time. I'm telling you. Either you marry me or I fight you for custody.'

Shock reverberated through Katie and she stared back at him. She could not immediately credit that he was serious. The last time she had been with Alexandros he had treated her like a lover, and now that warmth, trust and intimacy were gone, as though they had never been. 'I can't believe that you're threatening me.'

'Toby and Connor deserve better than what we're giving them. If I can give up my freedom, so can you.'

Her small hands curled into fierce fists. 'But what if I don't want to be your sacrifice?'

His golden gaze chilled. 'There's no scope for negotiation on this. I've already started making the wedding arrangements.'

Her green eyes flashed in angry disbelief. 'Well, then, you can just unmake them again.'

'Why would I do that? And why the big drama?' Alexandros delivered with derisive force. 'You're sleeping with me anyway, *glikia mou*!'

Katie turned scarlet. 'Don't you dare throw that in my face!'

Alexandros always went ice-cold in situations of conflict. But out of nowhere came a rage that could have lifted the roof off his vast Regency house. 'Throw what? The truth? If you'd been at home when I arrived today, you'd have gone to bed with me. Deny it if you can, but I don't think we need a line of expert witnesses to prove my point!'

The colour seeped back out of her cheeks to be replaced by pallor. She felt utterly humiliated. It was true. She had never been much good at saying no to him sexually, and she *would* have slept with him again. Being confronted by that mortifying fact cut her pride to ribbons. She refused to look at him and compressed her lips. 'Do you know where I was this morning? I had an interview for a job.'

'Do you spend *every* minute of your waking day figuring out how to wind me up?' Alexandros enquired in a raw, incredulous undertone, still struggling to suppress that disturbing surge of black fury that had taken hold of him. 'A job? Why is it your mission to reject everything I try to do for you?'

'All I'm trying to do is be independent—'

'Forget it. I never thought I'd say it, but we need to go back to old-fashioned basics. I don't want a caring, sharing partnership or an occasional lover. I want a wife. There are good reasons why we should marry, not the least being that we have two children and we very much like having sex,' Alexandros spelt out with sardonic bite. 'But the next time we share a bed, I'll be your husband.'

Katie lifted her chin. 'Would you really fight me for the twins in court?'

'If that's what it takes to bring you to your senses, *ne*…yes,' Alexandros declared without remorse. 'I think you're acting irresponsibly.'

'No, I'm not.'

'Maybe you're not mature enough yet to see what I see. Toby and Connor need stability and two parents. I know the worth of those advantages. I believe that I can make a difference in their lives, and that it is right that I should.'

Katie swallowed the thickness in her throat. She was furious with him. His threats outraged her sense of justice. Would he really try to separate her from the twins? Or was he just making a point? Did he appreciate or care what he was doing to her in the process? He wanted equal rights over his sons and a bigger say in what went on in their lives. If he was no longer prepared to compromise, only marriage would grant him those requirements.

Ironically, his refusal to continue taking a back seat role as a parent was not a total surprise to Katie. In recent months she had watched from the sidelines while Alexandros steadily grew from a reluctant father into a committed one. He had made a lot of effort to spend time with Toby and Connor, and as he got to know them he had learned to care for them. In fact, Alexandros had managed to form ties with his sons which were in no way dependent on her.

A sense of foreboding assailed Katie then. No longer could she view herself and her children as an indivisible threesome. Suddenly she was feeling very scared and insecure. Much more uncertainty hung over her own position in Alexandros's life. His sons would always be his sons, but she had no such safety of tenure. It was no consolation to acknowledge that she had last ended up in bed with him because she hadn't been able to contemplate the possibility that he might have an affair with someone else. In fact he had manipulated her into doing exactly what he wanted with shameless cold-blooded efficiency. He was very good at that. Achieving his objectives was what he did best. But what if he had now decided that it might make better sense to walk away and take the children with him? How much of a hold would sex give her when the novelty was beginning to wear off?

A trained observer, Alexandros could feel the tension emanating from Katie's slight, taut figure. He would say nothing that might lessen the pressure on her. Having reached a decision, he was convinced that he had to be cruel to be kind.

'I'm shocked that you should use threats to try and make me do what you want.' As Katie made that ringing condemnation her triangular face was very pale and her green eyes very bright.

Alexandros surveyed her steadily. 'No comment.'

'I won't forget this.' Swallowing the lump in her dry throat, Katie spun on her heel. 'I'll give you an answer tomorrow.'

The door flipped shut on her exit. Alexandros discovered that he wanted to smash something. She was so stubborn. She was the only woman he had ever met who was as stubborn as he was. What did she need to think about? He had laid it out plain and simple and with no avenue for escape. What was wrong with making an instant decision? Was she deliberately making him wait for an answer?

He poured a brandy. A job? Why was she applying for jobs? He raked an impatient hand through his cropped black hair and drank, wondering why she would never, ever do what he wanted—except in bed. He pictured her in an office environment. Someone as full of life and energy as Katie would be popular. She had a quick mind and an even quicker tongue. She worked hard, learned fast. She was very sexy....

He compressed his wide well-shaped mouth into a fierce and puritanical line. Just because *he* never hit on his staff— well, just that once, with her—it didn't mean other men were so scrupulous. More than one guy was likely to find her attractive, and would maybe think she was really up for it when they found out that she was already the mother of two children. In fact some men might even target her because of that background. He imagined the sexual wolves circling her when he was out of the country on business. His even white teeth gritted. He knocked back the brandy. He did not want that situation to develop.

Before he had realised that the woman in the bed in Katie's apartment wasn't actually Katie, he had come within inches of killing Damon Bourikas in cold blood. Bourikas was very lucky that he had kept his grimy paws off Katie Fletcher, for had it been otherwise Alexandros knew that he would not have let the younger man live to tell the tale. Alexandros had accepted that when it came to Katie he was possessive. He wanted to know that she was exclusively his, and that was why marriage was the only option he was now prepared to consider.

Katie ate a snack supper in her beautiful bedroom. She had little appetite for it, though. She was furious with Damon and her former nanny Maribel for what they had done, and deeply shaken that, in spite of all her care and caution on their behalf, her children had still been put at risk. She was hugely grateful that providence had brought Alexandros back to London early, and that he had caught the guilty couple out. How long might such behaviour have gone on behind her back without her finding out?

When she went to bed, she lay awake, torn by uncertainty and worry. But she had no doubts about the answer she had to give. For two very good reasons she *would* marry Alexandros. First and foremost, she could not afford to risk losing custody of her children. Alexandros would be a frighteningly rich and powerful opponent in the parenting stakes. If she fell out with him, made him an enemy, it could turn into a disaster. Suppose he simply took the children back to Greece and fought a court battle from his home turf? What rights would she have then? The fact that she loved Alexandros only got second billing in the reason corner, because just then she felt ashamed that she loved him. But he would soon learn that she had no intention of

condoning his use of duress by acting like a proper wife.
Oh, no, indeed, Katie reflected bitterly. He might win the
contest, but that did not mean he'd win all the usual spoils.

When Katie got up the next morning and discovered that
Alexandros had already left for London and the bank, as
though nothing had happened and it was another ordinary
working day, she was fit to be tied. Once she had dealt with
Toby and Connor's needs, she dialled his private number.

Alexandros dismissed the staff gathered round his desk
and mentally switched off from the major stockmarket
crisis that had forced him into the office at the crack of
dawn. '*Kalimera, pedhi mou,*' he greeted her lazily. 'I was
making plans for my stag night.'

Up until that point Katie had felt cool as a cucumber, but
the instant he said that, emphasising that he had never
doubted what her answer would be, she wanted to lunge
down the phone line and slap him. 'Not funny, Alexandros!'

Alexandros printed a K on the pad in front of him,
enclosed the letter in the jaws of a giant C, and circled it
for good measure. Temper as a response from Katie was
good, and it told him that he had her cornered. Success was
within reach. 'As busy as I am at present, a stag night looks
most unlikely. I thought a joke would lighten the mood.'

'Don't joke about what you said last night,' Katie told
him thinly. 'You didn't give me a choice, and that's the only
reason I'm going to marry you.'

'That's fantastic news,' Alexandros fielded, his intonation as confident and positive as though she had told him
she couldn't wait to see him at the altar. 'We'll go for a
special licence and get married in two weeks' time. The
wedding organiser will work with my staff, so that you can
concentrate your energies on choosing your dress.'

'No ideas to offer on that score?' Katie prompted,

tongue-in-cheek, since all the other arrangements and decisions already appeared to have been made.

'I would love to see you in white, *thespinis mou*. White from head to toe, no style statements. It'll be a very traditional wedding.' Alexandros jerked his head in frowning acknowledgement of the frantic pleading signals that two of his executives were giving him from the doorway. 'Look, I'm sorry, the helicopter is here to take me to the airport. I may not make it back much before the wedding, but I promise that I'll call you every day.'

The airport? Where was he going? She wanted to ask, but instead she was left with a dead phone humming and an attack of raging, screaming frustration. A few minutes later she switched on the business news and she found out about the stockmarket crisis.

CHAPTER NINE

TEARS of pride glimmering in her eyes, Maura Sullivan surveyed her daughter with a contented smile. An attractive woman with short copper hair, she looked a good deal younger than her fifty years. 'You look like a princess in a fairytale.'

'Honestly…? You're not just saying that?' Unconvinced, Katie studied her reflection in the elegant fitted gown, which clung with loving fidelity to her slender curves and made the most of her slim figure. The hand-embroidered fabric was gorgeous, but the design was plain, as she had decided that she did not have the height to carry anything more elaborate. A short, flirty crystal-beaded veil, attached to the exquisite diamond tiara which Calliope had insisted she borrow, added the final note.

'I know you're nervous because it's such a big fancy wedding, but Alexandros will only have eyes for you,' Maura declared with warm conviction. 'Dermot and I might only have met him last night, but we were very impressed with him. We weren't expecting someone so rich and important to be as friendly and welcoming.'

'Alexandros has buckets of charisma, and he was in top form yesterday,' Katie conceded, with the keen smile she wore every time she mentioned her bridegroom's name in her mother's presence; she didn't want the older woman worrying about her.

Maura had been thrilled at the news that her daughter was getting married, and Alexandros had phoned her in New Zealand to insist that she and Dermot, her second husband, make the trip to the UK at his expense. For Maura, one of the most enjoyable aspects of the entire affair had been the chance to meet her grandchildren and get to know them.

'It's an awful shame that business has kept you apart for the past fortnight, and then last night—when you must both have been gasping to be left alone—you had to entertain all your relatives and his.' Maura sighed with sympathy. 'But I must say, I do like his grandparents. They're just lovely people.'

'Yes,' Katie agreed fondly. Calliope and Pelias had provided her with sterling on-the-spot support, and the older couple's sincere delight in the wedding about to take place had touched her. At their insistence, Katie and her family had stayed in their spacious home in the run-up to the wedding.

Even so, nothing had so far managed to ease the tight, hard knot of angry hurt and insecurity that Katie was keeping hidden inside her. Thoughts that did nothing to lift her confidence continued to attack her. Ianthe's giant portrait, which still dominated the main staircase at Dove Hall, was a continual reminder of how uniquely impressive true physical beauty was. Either you were born with that blessing or you were born short with a nose like an elf's, Katie reflected bleakly. Whether she liked it or not, Alexandros was bound to be looking back today to his first wedding, and recalling how very different his feelings had been on that occasion. Ianthe had been loved and appreciated and grieved over, while Katie felt her children were of more importance to her bridegroom than she could ever be. Hers was to be a marriage of convenience, rather than love, and because he had already rejected her love once she would not offer it again.

'But I have to admit that I really don't know what you were doing when you decided to invite that Leanne Carson to your wedding,' Maura confided with a slight grimace. 'Did you get around to telling Alexandros about that yet?'

'No, I haven't. But Leanne was my friend, and if I want to forgive her for selling that trashy story to the newspaper, it's my business and nothing to do with him.'

'Well, you've always been very loyal to your friends, and I think that's great, but…' Maura hesitated uncomfortably. 'I wouldn't let Leanne cause trouble between you and Alexandros.'

'I'm giving her a second chance because she was always there for me when I was having a hard time.' Katie saw no reason to tell her mother that she wasn't actually planning to draw Alexandros's attention to Leanne's presence in the midst of several hundred guests. What he didn't know wasn't going to hurt him.

Katie had gone to visit Leanne on impulse. In truth, she had felt a great need to talk over the episode that had ruined their friendship. Leanne had been overjoyed to see her, and had apologised wholeheartedly for what she had done. When the other girl had admitted that she had only approached the journalist because she had been in fear of eviction after she'd fallen behind with her rent, Katie had understood, and had felt even more sympathetic.

At that point in her conversation with Maura, Katie's stepfather, Dermot Sullivan, came to tell them that it was time to leave for the church. A well-built man of medium height, he managed a car showroom in New Zealand. Maura's health and spirits had blossomed tremendously since her second marriage, and Katie liked the older man.

In less than two hours she would be Alexandros's second wife, Katie registered in a daze.

Toby and Connor and their new nanny, a sensible young woman in her thirties, with impeccable references, had already accompanied Alexandros's grandparents to the church. Getting into the white limousine, Katie was careful to keep her short train clear of the ground. The wedding didn't seem quite real to her, since Alexandros had been out of the country while everything was being organised, and her sole contact with him had been via the phone. Their conversations had been so stilted his grandparents could have listened to them and fallen asleep while Katie painstakingly described every minute of the twins' day and ignored enquiries that were the slightest bit more personal.

The night before, however, seeing Alexandros again after a break of two weeks had jolted her equilibrium, and she had been grateful that they were surrounded by other people. When Alexandros had attempted to speak to her alone, she had utilised every evasive tactic she knew and then vanished upstairs. From the landing above she had sneakily watched as Pelias intercepted his grandson before he could follow her.

Of one point Katie was certain: she was not letting Alexandros off the hook for what he had done. While she would act like a bride in public, she had no intention of carrying on the act in private. He had blackmailed her into marriage and he had had no business doing that. No way was she about to share a bed with a husband who had used the threat of a court custody battle to force her to the altar!

Alexandros needed to learn respect, and sleeping with him was clearly not the way to go about achieving that objective. The guy who had sworn he would fly round the world to spend an hour in bed with her was about to hear the word *no* for what might well be the first time in his life. Though she wasn't really looking forward to the moment when Alexandros finally realised how she intended to stand up for herself…

When she arrived at the Greek Orthodox church, Katie was totally disconcerted to find Alexandros waiting to greet her. Sheathed in a grey striped morning coat that was a superb fit, he looked devastatingly handsome. His dark golden eyes arrowed over her in intent appraisal as he presented her with an exquisite bouquet of flowers. 'It's a Greek tradition. You look very beautiful, *yineka mou*.'

'You're actually here to stay…no flight to catch?' Katie prompted sweetly, marvelling at the way in which he simply glossed over the blackmail he had employed to get her to the church. 'Nothing serious going down at the bank?'

Alexandros gave her an appreciative grin that proved the toughness of his hide and still made her heartbeat race. 'From today I'm all yours, and we're having a very long and very private honeymoon.'

The church interior had been beautifully decorated with flowers. Both she and Alexandros were handed a beribboned candle, and the service began. She knew exactly what was happening, because she had had the benefit of two separate meetings with the elderly priest, as well as a wedding rehearsal in which Pelias had stood in for his grandson with much humour. She and Alexandros exchanged rings. Symbolic matching crowns of silver and pearls joined by a ribbon were placed on their heads. They drank from the same cup of wine and circled three times the ceremonial table on which a bible sat. The guests showered them with rose petals. After the blessing the crowns were removed, and the priest joined their hands. It was a solemn and moving ceremony, and Katie discovered that even her anger with Alexandros could not detract from her awareness that they were now man and wife.

They left the church by a rear entrance, their arrival and their departure having gone unremarked by anyone other than the official photographer, a film crew and the security team. A huge number of precautions had been taken to preserve the privacy of the day. The invitations had requested that the guests take no photographs. Every detail of the arrangements had been kept hush-hush, and the reception was being staged at Dove Hall, where security was very tight to keep all members of the press outside the boundaries of the park.

In the wedding car, Alexandros settled an elaborate box on her lap. 'My wedding gift to you.'

Her green eyes sparked. 'What is it? A set of platinum handcuffs?'

Impervious to the possible existence of a sting in that comment, Alexandros lifted her hand and planted a kiss on her palm. Brilliant dark golden eyes set beneath sleek ebony lashes flicked over her with a sexual heat that took her by surprise. 'Would you like that, *thespinis mou*? But you're very small, and your skin would bruise easily,' he murmured huskily, lean brown fingers enclosing her slender wrist to emphasise the point. 'Silk would be kinder to such fragile bones.'

She felt a beetroot blush wash over her fair complexion and snatched her hand free, her skin tingling from his caressing touch. 'It was a joke…okay?'

'We'll see… Over the next eight weeks we will have time to explore a lot of uncharted territory.'

'*Eight* weeks?' Katie gasped, shock making her drop her

cool, frosty front. 'You're planning to take two months away from the bank?'

'It's a special occasion.' Alexandros tugged gently at a copper ringlet and let several more spill across his hand.

Suddenly she was feeling very much like an animated toy, being examined by a new owner, and her nervous tension raced up the scale at speed. When he found out that sex was not on the newly married menu, eight weeks would soon start feeling like seven weeks and six days too long. Now, however, was definitely not the time to make that announcement, for the very last thing she wanted to risk was the eruption of a row while they were surrounded by dozens of guests.

'How much time did you take off when you married Ianthe?' Katie heard herself ask with sudden curiosity.

A sharp silence fell and she held her breath.

'A week. There was no element of choice. I was about to sit my final exams at university.' His intonation was constrained, as if even talking about his first marriage was a painful challenge.

As well it might be to a male so reserved he hid all his emotions, Katie conceded unhappily. Wishing she hadn't asked, she addressed her attention to the still unopened box on her lap and flipped up the lid with an unsteady hand. 'Oh…my word…' she whispered, blinded by the radiance of an emerald and diamond ring.

'We didn't have an engagement…I want to make up for the fact,' Alexandros breathed gruffly.

Katie studied the ring, her hot gritty eyes glazing over with tears. Her heart felt as if it was cracking in two. In a sharp movement she closed the lid down again and stuffed the box back in his hand. 'I don't need a ring to remind me that you dumped me in Ireland!'

Alexandros almost groaned out loud. '*Theos mou*…that has nothing to do with this ring. Am I to live with these re-criminations for ever?'

Katie stared woodenly out of the window.

'I thought it was the wisest solution…I put what was best for you first.'

Katie slung him a withering glance. 'Don't kid yourself!'

'After Ianthe…I wasn't ready to make a commitment. I met you too soon. I felt guilty. You were very young and inexperienced—'

'Since when did that influence you?'

'You're the one and only virgin I've ever slept with!' Alexandros ground out furiously. 'If I'd taken you out of Ireland with me, what would I have been supposed to *do* with you?'

Katie elevated a delicate coppery brow in unashamed challenge. 'Oh, I'm sure you'd have thought of something.'

'The only future I was likely to have offered you then was as my mistress…that's why I ended it.'

'It is a far, far better thing that I do than I have ever done before?' Katie misquoted with lofty sarcasm. 'Why don't you just admit the truth? I told you I loved you, and the truth was such a turn-off that you left the country!'

Alexandros found it disturbing that she should have that much insight into the way he operated—particularly when he had not understood his own reactions half so well at the time.

While he was making that acknowledgement, Katie was struck by the level of her own bitterness, and mortified by what she had just said. What on earth was she playing at? The past was dead and gone. Some things—and unwelcome declarations of devotion fell very much into the category—were more sensibly left buried and forgotten. Alexandros had had an affair with her while he had still been grieving for Ianthe and she ought to have come to terms with that by now.

Regret swept over her. In a movement that was as abrupt as her former rejection of the gift, Katie swiped back the ring box from him. Thirty seconds later, she slid the gorgeous jewel onto the appropriate finger. 'Thank you... it's gorgeous,' she said, a tad flatly.

Alexandros was about to comment on that change of heart, and then decided not to look a gift horse in the mouth. It was a very big day for her, and she had had virtually no time to prepare for it. Possibly she was just feeling emotional, he reasoned, resolving to be supportive and understanding. He offered her a drink, asked her if her mother and stepfather were enjoying their trip, and then stuck so rigorously to making polite conversation that they travelled all the way to Dove Hall without a single opportunity arising for her to voice one more controversial word.

The wedding party took up position in the hall and greeted the guests as they filed past into the ballroom. Katie finally espied Leanne, a highly visible figure in her rather brief cerise satin dress, and tensed, hoping that her friend would manage to avoid attracting the bridegroom's notice. Sadly, it was not to be. Leanne, never one to hide her light or indeed anything else under a bushel, was determined to meet Alexandros. Stopping dead in front of him, she left Katie with no choice other than to make an introduction that she would have done just about anything to avoid.

'Leanne Carson...' Alexandros murmured, without any expression at all.

'I played cupid for the two of you,' the blue-eyed brunette proclaimed shamelessly. 'I mean, if it hadn't been for me, you and Katie might never have got together again! She was always very backward about coming forward.'

As Leanne passed on down the line, Katie could not bring herself to look at Alexandros. He inclined his proud dark head in a signal that brought Cyrus to his side, and a low-pitched exchange took place between the two men.

'You can't ask Leanne to leave when I invited her,' Katie whispered fiercely under her breath, fearing that that was his intent. 'I was going to tell you that she was here—'

'No, you weren't,' Alexandros shot back, cool as ice water dropping on a sizzling hotplate. 'You were hoping I wouldn't notice her in the crowd, but vulgarity of that magnitude is hard to miss!'

'What were you telling Cyrus?'

'To watch her...and the silver.'

'Thank you very much!'

Only when the last guests had arrived and they were about to enter the ballroom did Katie have the leisure to finally notice what she felt should have struck her the instant she entered the house. The huge portrait of Ianthe had been removed from above the main staircase and a pair of beautiful landscapes now hung in its place.

Thoroughly disconcerted by that development, she whispered, 'What did you do with Ianthe's portrait?'

The question made Alexandros glance at her in surprise. 'I had it moved.'

Katie almost thanked him, but when it occurred to her that doing so would be tantamount to confessing how sensitive she had been to the presence of that portrait, she embraced an awkward silence instead. Conscience told her that Ianthe had had every right to that place on the wall, and guilt writhed through her. How could she be so petty? Even so, she could not help but be impressed by her bridegroom's forethought and consideration on her behalf.

Reunited with Toby and Connor, she played with her sons for a few minutes, until it was time for her to join the bridal party at the high table.

She enjoyed a couple of glasses of champagne before
Alexandros took her on to the dance floor. When he drew
her close to his lean, hard body, she shivered a little.
Suddenly she was overwhelmingly aware of his potent
masculinity and how long it had been since they had last
been that close. The faint familiar aroma of his skin envel-
oped her, and she tensed in dismay at the flicker of sensual
heat curling low in her pelvis.

'Aren't you going to say anything more about Leanne?'
she queried, happy to offer that potential bone of conten-
tion in an effort to distract herself from a response that she
knew she had to suppress.

'Why did you invite her?'

'She's very sorry, and she was a friend for a long time.'
Her words muffled against his shoulder, Katie linked her
arms round his neck until she realised what she was doing.

'I hope you don't live to regret it. You're very trusting.
Some will take advantage of that trait and make it a weakness,' Alexandros warned her wryly. 'When someone lets
me down, I don't give them the chance to do it again.'

The movement of the dance brought him up against her,
ensuring that she was fully acquainted with the lithe
strength and power of his hard, muscular frame. Her mouth
ran dry. Her body seemed to have a series of triggers,
which responded without her mental output and made concentration an outrageous challenge.

As the music segued into another song, Alexandros
tugged her head back and gazed down at her with slumberous golden eyes. 'I can't wait to be alone with you. My
grandfather wouldn't even let me come up and talk to you
last night,' he confided hoarsely. 'Admittedly talking
wasn't much on my mind…'

Colour stung her cheekbones. She didn't know what to

say, and was entirely disconcerted when he lowered his proud dark head and tasted her generous pink lips with an intoxicating sensuality that left her head swimming and her knees weak.

Laughing appreciatively at the applause that had broken out from their audience, Alexandros brushed her flushed cheekbone with a long forefinger. 'Later…a wedding night to remember for a lifetime, *thespinis mou.*'

Katie veiled her eyes, feathery lashes concealing her troubled expression. Why was she feeling guilty? For goodness' sake, was loving Alexandros so deeply rooted in her psyche that she could deny him nothing? Even when he was very much in the wrong? She had been weak too often with Alexandros, and this was the reckoning time, she thought apprehensively. It was not a matter of trying to level the score. How could it be? Alexandros was her husband, and naturally she wanted a future with him. But it had to be a future in which she was more than the twins' mother and the woman in his marital bed. He might never love her, but she was determined that he should learn to treat her as an equal, a wife worthy of his respect.

As the afternoon wore on, however, it started to dawn on her that, in public at least, Alexandros did treat her very much as an equal. He had never been so attentive. He never once left her side while they worked their way round their guests. On more than one occasion he reminded those who wanted to talk business with him that it was his wedding day.

When the bride and groom had satisfied the conventions, they sat down with Toby, Connor, Maura and Dermot for a while. That was the moment when their younger son, Connor, chose to haul himself up on the edge of a sofa and take his first wobbling steps towards his mother. His little face lit up with amazement at the achievement of walking upright for the very first time.

'Aren't you wonderful?' Dropping down on her knees, Katie opened her arms wide and caught Connor to her in an exuberant hug. She saw the same glow of love and pride in Alexandros's lean dark face. A lump formed in her throat when she watched him comfort Toby, who had tried and failed to emulate his brother's feat and burst into floods of tears.

Pelias joined her later, when she was helping to put the children down for a much-needed nap. 'Calliope is so excited about having Toby and Connor to stay with us this week. Of course we'll have your nanny to help out, but we have so many treats planned. When they wake up, we'll take them.'

'I'm going to miss the little rascals,' Katie confided ruefully. 'But it *is* only for a week.'

The bridal couple were to spend their wedding night at Dove Hall and leave for their Greek honeymoon the following day.

'A week for the grown-ups to enjoy being newly married and alone.' Pelias Christakis studied her with warm approval. 'I had almost given up hope of seeing it happen, but you have transformed my grandson's life.'

'I've turned it upside down,' Katie slotted in ruefully.

'Alexandros deserves a normal marriage and family life. We are sincerely happy for you both,' Pelias told her gruffly.

As she went back downstairs, that phrase, *a normal marriage*, made her a frown. It seemed an odd thing for Pelias to have said. Had it been a veiled criticism of his grandson's first marriage? Doubtless it had been a reference to Ianthe's infertility. Children, after all, were highly prized in Greek culture. But she was still a little surprised, for all things considered it had been a rather unkind comment—and Pelias Christakis was one of the kindest, most tactful men she had ever met.

Cyrus approached her. 'Leanne Carson is taking photos with her phone,' he informed her.

Katie blinked, and the pink bled out of her cheeks. 'Are you sure?'

The older man nodded confirmation.

'Does…my husband know?'

'Mr Christakis said that you would want to deal with it.'

Her tummy knotted at the prospect of that unpleasant challenge, but accompanied by Cyrus, she went downstairs to confront her friend. Leanne just laughed when reminded that there had been an embargo on photos printed on her invitation. The phone was a very expensive high-tech model. Katie suspected that the other woman had deliberately come armed with the means to invade their privacy and that of their guests. Was some newspaper already standing by, waiting to hear from her?

Leanne needed little encouragement to show off the pictures she had taken, and Katie was horrified to see that the twins featured—as well as certain celebrity guests caught unawares. Leanne only lost her temper when Katie passed the phone to Cyrus to delete the photos. A car was already waiting to take the furious brunette to the train station. Her vindictive final comments hurt Katie more than anything else that had taken place, and she was seriously worried that another newspaper article might appear. Had Leanne managed to send any of the photos before their deletion? And would a tell-all scoop of a story appear in print regardless? After all, Leanne would still be able to describe their entire wedding day.

Alexandros said nothing. Unaware of what had taken

place, Pelias and Calliope took their leave with Toby, Connor and the nanny. Maura and Dermot left next, and Katie hugged her mother close. Her mother and stepfather were planning to spend a week visiting friends and relatives before flying back to New Zealand.

Soon the steady hum of cars and helicopters marked the departure of the guests, and the bride's tension began to climb like a pressure gauge. As the moment of revelation with regard to their wedding night came closer, Katie could feel her store of courage shrinking.

'Where are you going?' Alexandros asked when he saw her near the top of the staircase.

'Well…er…to get changed,' she mumbled through stiff lips, all composure threatening to desert her.

'But why?' Alexandros mounted the stairs to join her on the landing. He closed light hands to her shoulders and turned her away from the direction in which she had been about to head. 'Our bedroom is this way, *agape mou.*'

'It's been a really, really lovely day…'

As Leanne's shocking behaviour swam back into Katie's memory like a giant man-eating shark, she was silenced. She waited for Alexandros to make a sardonic comment on that same score but he did not.

'The very best…' Alexandros agreed, with remarkable restraint.

With careful hands he turned her back to face him and then bent down and swept her up into his arms.

'What on earth are you doing?' Katie gasped.

'I like the fact you're mine, lock, stock and barrel now,' Alexandros shared, striding down the corridor and shouldering his passage into a room bedecked with so many glorious flowers that her jaw dropped as he lowered her to the carpet. 'Calliope flew in Greek florists. She really goes for all the traditional stuff. This is a mark of her affection for you. But I told her not to bother rolling a baby on the bed…'

'I beg your pardon?' Katie echoed weakly.

'It's another tradition. But fertility is not one of our problems.' Laughing huskily, Alexandros drew her back into the shelter of his big, powerful body. 'I love our sons, but I would like to wait a little while before we extend the family. I want my precious wife all to myself,' he breathed thickly.

Within the strong circle of his arms, Katie felt as at risk as a bale of straw within reach of a match. She had still to drag her mesmerised attention from the bed, which had been transformed into a romantic floral bower. It was all so gorgeous—but now she had to say what she had to say, and he was going to hate her…

Easing free of his light hold, Katie spun round and backed off a couple of steps. 'I have something I have to say to you…'

His breathtaking smile lit his lean, strong features and made her heart hammer like a road drill. 'And I have something I have to say to you.'

'Me first,' Katie countered hurriedly, keen to get her little speech over with. 'I'm not going to sleep with you tonight. Now, please don't get mad about that.'

Alexandros had gone very still. Dense black lashes dipped almost to his stunning cheekbones, then slowly lifted again on glittering golden eyes filled with level enquiry. 'This is our wedding night. Why would you decide not to sleep with me?'

Katie closed her hands tightly in on themselves. 'Because you blackmailed me into marrying you, and that was wrong.'

'Blackmail is an evocative word. I wanted to marry you, and I cut through all the…nonsense.' Alexandros selected that final word with care, and squared his stubborn jawline. 'And here we are, married and with our whole lives before us. Please don't tell me that you're planning to destroy that.'

Katie made a tiny movement with a jerky hand, her normal relaxed motion restricted by the reality that the level of tension in the room was truly horrendous. 'I'm not planning to destroy anything—'

'Then why give me grounds for divorce on our wedding night?' Alexandros demanded wrathfully 'What *is* all this?'

CHAPTER TEN

ANGER burnishing his challenging gaze, Alexandros was unable to wait for her to answer that demand for clarity. 'This is some petty revenge because I saw what was right for us and I went for it on my own. You didn't like my methods?' he queried. 'Tough. My methods get results. If I'd left you in charge, we'd still be in limbo and nothing would be decided!'

'Well, it's good to know that your conscience won't be keeping you awake at night,' Katie responded, fighting the fact that her nerves had gone into panic mode at that reference to divorce. 'You need to accept that what you did was wrong, Alexandros—'

'How's it *wrong*? You're my wife now. My children will take on my name—'

'I want our relationship to be about *us*, not about the children—'

'Then stop behaving like a child!'

Katie breathed in deep, mentally buckled herself into defensive armour and held up a finger. '*One*…I married you because you threatened to contest my custody of the kids—'

'I wouldn't have done that to you!' Alexandros grated,

with a flash of his even white teeth. 'Don't you know *anything* about me yet?'

'*Two*—'

'*Siopi*…quiet!' Alexandros cut in. 'Holding up fingers and counting is bloody irritating.'

'*Two*…' Katie launched defiantly. 'I don't want to sleep with a guy who makes me feel that I'm only good enough for sex!'

'I don't want to sleep with a wife who thinks that she can use her body like a bargaining chip!'

'*Three*,' Katie continued doggedly. 'I—'

Alexandros threw up both hands in an explosive demonstration of rage. 'I'm out of here!'

'No…don't be like that!' Katie gasped, racing past him at breakneck speed to plant her back against the door and block his exit.

'Move.'

'But we need to talk—'

'I'm not in the mood. Move.'

'No…'

In response, Alexandros scooped her up off her feet, crossed the room in two strides and dumped her down on the bed. He came down over her and she lay there, looking up at him with huge green eyes full of surprise and uncertainty. 'Alexandros…'

'When you say my name it's an invitation.' Tawny eyes smouldering gold with aggression, he took her lips with a passionate urgency that melted her body into a honeyed compliancy that tore giant holes in her defences.

With a sob of regret in her throat, Katie pulled free.

Alexandros surveyed her with a savage condemnation that seemed to her to be all out of proportion to what she had done. His lean bronzed face might have been chipped out of granite, and he was pale below his dark skin.

'I swore I'd never marry again. I changed for you. I swore I'd never have children. I learned to accept and love our sons,' he breathed, with a bleakness of tone that made her break out in a sweat. 'And I thought you were different. Loving and giving and truthful. Well, where the hell has that all gone?'

His fierce bitterness cut through every layer of her skin. Suddenly she felt very much in the wrong, even if she did not quite comprehend exactly what that wrong was. What she did grasp was that in his eyes she had let him down, betrayed him, and that accusation hurt like hell. Who had he thought she was different *from*? She had never seen him reveal that much emotion before, and it shook her inside out.

The door closed. He was gone. She had done what she'd set out to do. She had stood firm, stuck like glue to her convictions. But she had not got to state the finer points of what she had intended to say. However, she had got across the basic message, she reminded herself, and, considering the hostility of her audience, that had been quite an achievement.

Her muscles were aching with the stiffness of extreme stress. Slowly, clumsily, she flopped back in her floral bower. She was still clad in her exquisite dress and tiara. *He* would have taken them off. Without any warning at all, she was racked by the most terrible doubts, and the tears started flowing.

The next day, Katie went down to breakfast at eight.

At one in the morning she had gone looking for Alexandros. Searching a house that contained two hundred and thirty two rooms had ultimately become too much of an embarrassing challenge as she'd run into or disturbed various members of the household staff. She'd rung his mobile, but it was switched off. Even if she had run him to earth, she had no idea what she would have said to him, and feared that, in the mood he had been in, she might actually have made things worse.

During the night, she had not slept a wink. She'd lain awake, hoping that Alexandros might come back to talk to her, and fretting herself to death when she had been left in splendid isolation. Suppose Alexandros demanded a divorce? Suppose he had left the country? Would he even go ahead with the honeymoon now?

She had got up at six to double-check her packing, then spent ages trying to hide the redness of her eyes with make-up. She'd put on a green skirt and top that she wasn't that fussed about but had bought purely because he liked her in short skirts.

The dining room was empty. She comfort-ate her way through a huge breakfast.

The wave of relief that assailed her when Alexandros strolled in, casually elegant in beige cargo pants and an Italian knit sweater, left her dizzy.

'Are you ready?' he asked.

A second wave of relief washed over her; the honeymoon was still on the travel schedule.

'Like the skirt,' he murmured, as she clambered with the greatest difficulty into the limo.

'Are you still talking to me?'

'Got any more skirts like that in your luggage?'

'Alexandros—'

He leant over and rested a silencing finger against her soft pink mouth. 'No—don't say it again, *agape mou*. "We need to talk" has to qualify as the phrase most likely to make the average guy run like hell.'

Green eyes huge, she nodded slowly. He lounged back into his corner, contriving to look absolutely gorgeous. She swallowed hard. They *did* need to talk, but now she was too scared to risk it. The night before he had told her that he had changed for her, and that declaration had shocked her, giving her another, not entirely welcome perspective of their relationship. Did he mean that marrying her and learning to be a father had been major sacrifices? She reckoned that he might well do, and she felt cut to the bone. There she was, always asking for more from him, and she knew that that was unfair and unreasonable.

A large contingent of the press awaited them at the airport. They were kept at a distance by Cyrus and his men. Alexandros closed a protective arm round Katie and ignored the questions flying their way. Someone said something about 'the latest story' and her blood went cold. *What story?* She cringed at the idea that Leanne's revelations might have made it into print again, and started praying feverishly. She could not work up the courage to ask Alexandros.

They boarded his private jet. She saw the neat rows of newspapers on the desk and riffled through them, to emerge with the trashiest—which bore a rather grainy depiction of them kissing on the dance floor.

Alexandros rested a lean brown hand over hers before she could lift the publication. 'Don't waste your time,' he advised.

But Katie was a glutton for punishment. She leafed through to find the centre spread. As far as embarrassing photos went, there was only one more, showing her in her bridal finery, but every detail of their special day was now public knowledge. Her eyes watered like mad and she stared into space, fighting for self-control. She felt so terribly to blame. She had been stupid and sentimental to trust Leanne again.

'I'm sorry about this,' she mumbled tightly.

'Forget it.'

But his forbearance was too much for her. Before the tears could overflow, she told him that she was going to lie down, and fled into the sleeping compartment. Sitting on the side of the bed, she struggled to hold the sobs back. The door opened thirty seconds later.

Alexandros sat down beside her and tugged her back against him. 'It's no big deal.'

'Everyone went to so much trouble and expense trying to keep our wedding private, and I blew it all sky-high!' Katie sobbed. 'I shouldn't have invited her—'

'You thought she was your friend.'

'That's what hurts…'

'Shush…' Alexandros sighed. 'I know.'

'Why aren't you furious with me?'

'I like the fact that you're like a chocolate with a soft centre,' he confided. 'If you were as tough as I am, you wouldn't be the same person, *agape mou*.'

She gulped in oxygen. 'Why are you being so nice?'

'I wasn't nice last night?'

A choked laugh was dredged from her, and she squirmed round to curl more intimately into the solid heat and strength of him. Love was running through her like a riot, and lust was following a close second. She was his, absolutely his, at that moment. She shifted closer, the tips of her breasts rubbing against the solid wall of his chest.

Alexandros reached down and straightened a pillow. He edged her away from him and slowly lowered her head down on to it. 'You're exhausted. You should get some sleep.'

'Where were you last night?' she whispered.

'Getting drunk.'

'Oh…' Katie just could not imagine that. And, knowing how much he liked to stay in control, could only feel that she had driven him into an act that was out of character.

'For what it's worth,' Alexandros announced from the doorway, lean, strong face grim, 'you were right about the blackmail. It was cruel. It was wrong. And I make no excuses. I knew what I was doing. I wasn't prepared to do the courtship thing…I wasn't even sure I *could* do it…I just wanted it—you and I—sorted.'

Katie wondered what 'the courtship thing' might have entailed. He had wanted it sorted? Yes, she understood that. He was very impatient, very stubborn, and very dominant—particularly in any field where he believed that he knew best.

'What do we do next?' she whispered.

'The honeymoon.'

Alexandros owned a private island. They flew in on a helicopter, which he piloted himself. From the air he showed her a sprawling white house, set in wooded ground above a white stretch of beach, and flew across the island to let her see the village. Down in the harbour, a ferry had docked. As they turned to head back inland a fisherman waved from a brightly coloured blue boat.

'We'll spend the rest of the week here, and then, if you feel like something more lively, we'll hit Ibiza at the weekend.'

At the house, cushioned wicker seating furnished the tiled terrace below stone arches that looked out to sea. The freshwater infinity pool shared the same incredible view. Decorated in Mediterranean blue and white shades that took on amazing clarity in the clear light, the interior of the house was pure enchantment. Rustic antiques were set off by natural cotton draperies and inviting sofas. And beyond the characterful charm and simplicity lay marble bathrooms to die for and a kitchen that a world-class chef would not have disdained.

'I love it…I really love it.'

Alexandros settled her luggage down in the fabulous master bedroom. 'As do I…it's always been a special place for me.'

Had he brought Ianthe to the island? Intelligence told her that he most probably had, and she scolded herself for being envious of a dead woman. But still she fell victim to mental images of the exquisite Ianthe posing out on the veranda, or draped elegantly across an opulent sofa, while Alexandros watched with helpless admiration.

They dined by candlelight on the terrace, and she sipped champagne. She wore the emerald and diamond ring and flaunted it as much as she dared. She had noticed that he was not touching her, and he hadn't put his luggage in the same room. Suddenly being apart from him felt really dangerous. If the distance between them got too great, maybe she would lose him altogether, she thought feverishly. All her insecurities were steadily mounting to the surface.

'Why won't you talk about Ianthe?' she asked him abruptly, and she really hadn't meant to say it. But there the controversial subject was, out on the table, like a giant rock suddenly surfacing from a clear sea.

Alexandros frowned in surprise and the silence stretched. He thrust back his chair and stood up. 'Why *would* I talk about her?'

Her nerves on edge, Katie forced a rueful smile. 'You were with her for the best part of a decade.'

Lean, darkly handsome face taut, Alexandros vented a sardonic laugh. 'And perhaps that's something I'd prefer to forget.'

That suggestion hung there while she gaped at him with steadily widening green eyes. 'Are you…? I mean, what you just said…er…I don't understand,' she fumbled shakily, unable to believe what he had just implied.

Alexandros shook his handsome dark head in apparent wonderment. 'Are honeymoons always this bad?'

Katie froze, and turned pale as milk.

Without another word, Alexandros strode off in the direction of the beach.

After a moment of paralysis, Katie scrambled up and chased after him, kicking off her high-heeled sandals to plunge into the soft sand in his wake. It was a clear night, and the full moon was shedding a lot of light. 'You can't blame me for being curious. You didn't tell me about her in Ireland, when we first met, and later, when I wanted to know more about her, you told me that I didn't have the right to know anything about your marriage!' she reminded him in a feverish rush.

'That was way back at the beginning. In Ireland I had no reason to talk about her. I knew you would be upset if you knew I'd been married and, like most men, I avoided the issue. I don't talk about her because I don't want to.'

'But I thought that if you'd really loved someone and lost them you'd want to talk about it…at least sometimes. Wouldn't that be healthier?'

'It wasn't like that between Ianthe Kalakos and I.' Alexandros stuck his hands deep in his pockets and stared out to sea, his bold, bronzed profile bleak.

'Then please tell me how it was,' Katie muttered. 'I really need to know.'

'I was twenty years old. She was twenty-four. My friends thought she was gorgeous, and they all said how lucky I was when she set her sights on me. She was up for anything, and at that age that was all I needed. I thought it was a casual thing. She said it was too. I was about to finish it when she told me she was pregnant.' Hearing Katie gasp, he turned his dark head and said grimly, 'Been there, done that, got the T-shirt…is that what you're thinking? It didn't turn out to be that simple, *thespinis mou.*'

But what he had already told her seemed to explain so much that Katie was knocked for six. He had been through the unplanned pregnancy scenario long before she came along with the twins. No wonder he had been so reluctant to credit that it could happen to him again. Lightning, it seemed, *could* strike twice in the same place. 'What happened?'

'I didn't even hesitate… I was a well-brought-up Greek boy. I married her, made two families very happy. A month after the wedding I accompanied Pelias to London for a business meeting, and when I got home Ianthe told me she had lost the baby.'

Katie winced. 'I'm so sorry.'

'Don't be. Ianthe was immediately determined to have a baby to replace the one she said she'd lost. I wasn't as keen. I was too young. But, had a child been born, I would have done my best. I did try to be as supportive of her needs as I could be. Five years after the marriage we were still childless, and I went with her to see her latest consultant because I was concerned by the weird treatment she was having. Quite accidentally I learned that she had never been pregnant in her life.'

Katie pressed a hand to her parted lips. 'Oh, my word… she lied to you about having conceived?'

'All that time we'd been living her lie. I couldn't believe that I'd been such an idiot. I was too naive to even *think* of asking her for proof before I agreed to marry her.' Alexandros sighed.

'You know…I imagined that you had had the perfect marriage with Ianthe,' Katie whispered apologetically.

'On the surface it did look perfect to a lot of people. Ianthe didn't have close friends, and our marriage *was* a perfect fantasy in her mind. But when I found out that she'd lied about the pregnancy, I told her I wanted a divorce…and she responded by trying to kill herself.'

'Oh, no…' Katie gasped in horror.

'That was when I realised that Ianthe wasn't really responsible for what she did. She was unstable—a fantasist who was obsessed with me,' he admitted, with a bleakness of tone that made her tummy clench. 'She couldn't bear to be on her own, and never stopped telling me how much she loved me.'

'And you felt trapped.' Katie was finally realising why such declarations weren't his style. Damon Bourikas had remarked that Alexandros had become a workaholic after his marriage. She imagined he had used work as an escape from the pressure of a relationship that must always have demanded more than he was able to give. For someone with his reserved nature, such emotional histrionics must have been an even greater challenge.

'I *was* trapped. She was my wife and my responsibility. Her parents were dead by then. I got her psychiatric treatment, but it didn't make much difference. She'd act a little more grounded for a while, and then slide back. She was taking heavy-duty medication when she crashed her car. She wasn't even supposed to be driving.'

The silence lay there until Katie finally picked up the courage to ask what she still longed to know. 'Did you ever love her?'

He released his breath on a stark hiss. 'No…not for a single moment.'

Katie blinked back hot stinging tears. 'I've been horribly

jealous of her, and yet she must've been so unhappy—and so must you have been.'

'When she died I felt incredibly guilty, because I knew I had my life back again and I'd wanted it back so badly I could taste it,' he grated in hoarse admission. 'I've never been able to forgive myself for that.'

'You did the best you could. You stuck by her,' Katie mumbled, half under her breath. 'Not every man would've done that in those circumstances. How much do your grandparents know about this?'

'Very little. But they must've had their suspicions that things weren't right. It was better that I didn't talk about it, though. It was easier to just do what I had to do and protect Ianthe by keeping up a front,' Alexandros told her flatly. Do you mind if I go for a walk?'

The abruptness of that request unbalanced her at a moment when all her concentration was focused on him. There was so much more she would have liked to have asked and said.

'No, of course not,' she lied, and headed straight back to the house. He wanted to be alone, and she was willing to bet that that had been a problem when Ianthe was around. Obsessive love was possessive, demanding and suffocating. His first marriage had been a nightmare that had to have poisoned his past with Katie and their present. How could it not have done? Of course he was wary of female love, expectations and commitment after such a ghastly experience. He had lost years of his life to a deeply troubled woman, and yet he had behaved with great honour. She realised in surprise that she loved him all the more for not having let Ianthe down. Yet in choosing not to confide even in Pelias and Calliope he had added to his burden of stress.

To have something to do she cleared up the dinner dishes, even though staff would come in the following day to take care of the housework. She went to bed but left her lamp lit, reckoning that it would show under the door. An hour later she heard him come back. She listened to the faint sound of the shower running next door and waited to see if he would come to her.

She lay in bed thinking about Alexandros and the state of their marriage. Not good, she concluded fearfully. He had admitted that he should not have used coercive tactics to get a wedding ring on her finger. How was withdrawing all intimacy likely to improve their relationship? Wouldn't it push them apart? He was so passionate. Why hadn't she thought of that? He had finally talked to her about Ianthe and she understood a lot of things much better now. In committing to marry a second time, he had made a much bigger leap in faith than she could ever have appreciated.

Confrontational demands did not seem much of a reward for that leap. She worried at her full lower lip and glanced at her watch. It was obvious that he was not about to join her—and why would he when she had said she would not sleep with him? Before she could lose her nerve, she got up again.

Alexandros was stretched out on the bed with his hands laced above his head, the sheet riding low on his hard flat stomach.

Moonlight revealed the wide-awake gleam of his gaze and Katie leant back against the door, her heart thumping like mad inside her. 'It's me…'

'What can I help you with?' he enquired lazily

Her face flamed, making her glad of the low level of the light. 'S-sex,' she stammered.

Alexandros resisted an unholy urge to grin and punch

the air in triumph. A suffering shared was a suffering halved. 'Come here...'

Anchoring a hand into her silky ringlets, he dragged her mouth hungrily down to his. She moaned under that urgent onslaught, heat pooling like liquid gold between her slender thighs.

He cupped her cheekbones between spread fingers. 'I can't think about anything or anyone but you, *thespinis mou*.' He dipped his tongue provocatively between her lips and eased her out of her nightdress.

'Neither can I...'

When she was all of a quiver with intense anticipation, he paused. 'Promise me you'll put on your wedding dress for me tomorrow, so that I can take it off...'

In a daze, she looked down at him, not quite sure she had heard him right. He ran a caressing hand over the swollen peaks of her breasts. Her stark indrawn breath was audible. 'I didn't bring it with me.'

'I'll organise a special delivery.' Binding her slender body to his hair-roughened muscular chest with a strong arm, Alexandros sat up and murmured in earthy challenge, 'So, wife of mine...will you dress up for me if I ask?'

'Yes...'

'You philistine,' he whispered huskily. 'How could you call anything this sublime just *sex*?'

So shamelessly excited she couldn't think straight, Katie closed her eyes beneath his demanding mouth and revelled in the tide of his hungry passion.

Four weeks later, Katie parked down at the harbour in her four-wheel-drive. She was early, so she lifted Toby and Connor out of their seats and buckled them into the light buggy she always carried in the boot. Her sons struggled against their harnesses and complained. Every since they had begun to learn to walk they had grown increasingly less tolerant of such restraint on their movements.

'Behave,' she told them sternly, copying the tone that Alexandros used when his sons played up.

'Mum-mum,' Toby murmured in a pathetic tone, all big brown eyes and charm.

Connor just stuck out his arms and gave her a big hopeful smile.

Helpless love surging through her, Katie crouched down and hugged each one in turn. A slim bright figure in a turquoise sundress, she walked up the village street. Several old people sat out on chairs at the front of their homes, and some children were playing with a ball. She smiled and responded to greetings, pausing now and then to allow the boys to be admired. She made liberal use of the Greek phrases Alexandros had taught her, and was delighted whenever she managed to add to her vocabulary.

She had a soft drink in the taverna, and sat out in the evening sunlight, enjoying the glorious view of the sea and the wonderful sense of relaxation she had. Alexandros did honeymoons really well. Just to think that she had another four weeks of the same bliss to look forward to made her feel positively giddy. He had already taken her shopping and clubbing and sailing and fishing.

The first week had been filled with lazy sun-drenched days when they had never been apart for more than a moment. Nothing had ever been so intense for her. She had never dreamt that she could feel as close to him as she now did, or that he could be so tender and affectionate. The barriers had come down after he'd told her the truth about Ianthe. The only time she had seen that cool reserve of his since was when some tourists had come ashore to stage a raucous party on their private beach.

Indeed, Katie had never been so happy in all her life. They had talked endlessly about so many things—even what it had been like for her when she was pregnant. That she had had to undergo that experience alone still bothered him. He was so good to her. She had bought designer clothes in Corfu town and modelled them for him. She was steadily acquiring a collection of contemporary jewellery. She fingered an earlobe, newly healed from being pierced to carry exquisite platinum and pearl earrings. She had been rather nervous, but he had held her hand through that experience. He spoiled her. He kept her awake at night in all sorts of infinitely fascinating and seductive ways. She was more madly in love with Alexandros Christakis than ever.

She watched his yacht skimming in and sailing into the harbour with sure skill. Alexandros appeared, and his crewman vaulted lithely on to the jetty to tie the craft up. Relief filled her. She wasn't into fishing, so that was the one thing he got to do alone. But, even though the sea had been smooth as glass all day, she could never quite relax until he came back again.

Evening sunlight providing pleasant warmth on her back, she walked down to the harbour to greet him. Clad in disreputable cargo shorts and a black T-shirt, Alexandros uncoiled his lithe, powerful frame from the yacht. He needed a shave, and it made him look like a very sexy pirate. She felt that little clenching sensation deep down inside her that only he could evoke, and stilled.

His beautiful eyes glittered, and he lowered his tousled dark head to kiss her with long, slow, intoxicating sweetness. He jerked back from her and looked down in surprise.

Toby was hauling on the hem of his shorts to demand his father's attention.

'I'm kissing your mother…have some pity,' Alexandros censured, reaching back for Katie.

Belatedly aware of the amused looks their amorous behaviour was attracting, Katie backed off and began to unclip her sons from the buggy. 'Let's go home.'

'It's such a long way…and I hate waiting, *agape mou*,' Alexandros growled, pressing his sensual mouth hotly to the nape of her neck as her ringlets cascaded over to one side.

Katie went breathless. Having watched him stow their sons in the four-wheel drive, she got in. 'What does it mean?' she asked across the bonnet.

'What does what mean?'

'*Agape mou…*'

Alexandros sprang into the driver's seat. In the silence, thinking that perhaps he hadn't heard her, she repeated the question and pointed out that he used the expression a lot.

He drove off. His handsome mouth compressed, he shrugged. 'It means…my love. That's all.'

Katie's eyes opened to their fullest extent. She dared not look at him. He'd sounded so dismissive of the endearment that it was clearly just an expression. Had her question made him uncomfortable? He said not a word all the way back along the twisting road that led to the house. Their smiling nanny emerged to take charge of Toby and Connor, and Alexandros gripped Katie's hand and dragged her into the house.

Giggling and blushing as he urged her into their bedroom and kicked shut the door behind him, she protested, 'Alexandros…'

'There's been something I've been meaning to say to

you...' Alexandros incised tautly. 'It's your own fault I didn't say it on our wedding day.'

Dismayed by his tone and tension, Katie whispered, 'Say what? *What* was my fault?'

His lean dark face clenched, lashes sweeping down as he studied the floor. 'I just feel so stupid saying it. I love you...okay? Right? I fell in love with you in Ireland, but I didn't recognise it for what it was. My emotions were so strong that I couldn't believe it was normal to feel that way.'

Katie blinked. 'Are you serious?' she mumbled dizzily.

'Yes. It was very destabilising stuff.'

Katie was honestly afraid she would faint with shock. 'Destabilising?'

'There I was, working at getting over a bad marriage, and then in you walked. I went straight off the rails into territory I didn't know even existed,' he admitted in a driven undertone. 'I'm the guy who plans everything, and nothing that happened with you was planned. I didn't realise it was love. I thought it was my unbalanced state of mind after Ianthe's death...that I was upset, out of control.'

'Our timing wasn't very lucky. So you loved me,' she conceded, striving to adjust to what he was telling her but very challenged to do so. 'No wonder I was so devastated when it all ended. I'd felt so sure of you up until that point...'

His dense lashes lifted on his brooding golden gaze and there was a definite appeal there for her understanding. 'When you told me you loved me, all I could think about was Ianthe. It was not that you reminded me of her in any way. But her confessions of love that I could never return still haunted me then.'

'Maybe you needed that time to get over what had happened with Ianthe. Were you really going to tell me you loved me on our wedding day?'

'You blew it,' he reminded her ruefully. 'You told me the wedding night was off.'

'It would have been full speed ahead if you'd mentioned love! When did you find out that you loved me?'

'I ignored my sneaking suspicions until the day I went into your apartment and thought for all of thirty seconds that it was you, rather than the nanny, who was shagging Damon Bourikas. Suddenly my mental fog cleared,' Alexandros confessed raggedly. 'The belief that you might have found consolation with another man almost killed me...almost killed *him* too.'

'My goodness, is that why you pulled the blackmail thing to get me to marry you?'

Alexandros nodded warily.

'Oh, that's so sweet.' Katie hugged him, thinking that fear of losing her was an award-winning excuse. 'And the picnic I rubbished. It was more real than I could've appreciated.' Her mind continued to rove over the blanks, and now she had him talking she had no intention of holding back any questions. 'But why did you keep on harping on about how it was just sex?'

'At first I thought it was, and then it seemed safer to keep it on that level—'

'You almost broke my heart!' Katie heard herself confess, and she was appalled, but a great surge of emotion had welled up inside her and a strangled sob emerged.

Alexandros grabbed her with a satisfying lack of his usual cool. Apologising in Greek and English, he covered her damp face with comforting kisses. *'Signomi*...I'm sorry. I can't be happy without you. Nobody else can make me feel the way you do, yet until it was almost too late I didn't understand why.'

'You must have been really stupid!' she hissed in tearful condemnation.

Alexandros wrapped both his arms tightly round her and rocked her against him until she had calmed down. 'I know I don't deserve you, but I really do love you, *agape mou*. You and the children have brought me back to life and I wake up every day feeling blessed,' he swore gruffly.

She subsided against him and held him close. 'I love you too,' she whispered happily. 'I can finally say it again.'

'I'll never stop saying it, *agape mou*.'

'What a little precious,' Calliope Christakis sighed, peeping into the cot at her newest great-grandchild, a little girl named Athena. 'She's dainty, just like her mother. And to think you and my grandson said there would be no more children for a few years!'

Katie blushed and grinned. Athena was now three months old. Not much planning had gone into her conception. Alexandros had merely murmured one night that he would love to see her body ripen with his child, and birth control had been abandoned there and then. Athena had been on the way within weeks.

Toby and Connor were now three years old. Energetic and talkative pre-schoolers, the twins were thick as thieves when plotting mischief, but each had a distinctive personality. Toby was a quick-tempered livewire, Connor the more thoughtful and calm leader of the pair.

They had flown out to the villa in Italy with his grandparents only two days before. Pelias and Calliope, however, weren't staying for long on this occasion. The older couple were about to leave on an escorted tour of their favourite Italian cities. Leaving the children in the tender care of the staff, Katie strolled downstairs with Calliope and kissed her goodbye. She waved at Pelias, who was already waiting in the car and tapping his watch, shaking his head in teasing rebuke of his wife's tardiness.

Sometimes Katie found it hard to credit that she had been married for two whole years. Her mother and her stepfather had been over for a lengthy visit at the start of the summer. Alexandros made sure she saw her family as often as possible. He went out of his way to make her happy and she loved that in him. Their marriage had gone from strength to strength as their trust in each other blossomed and added a sense of warm mutual security. They both very much valued what they had together.

Alexandros had taken some drastic measures to cut down on his working hours. That had not been easy for him, and at first she and the twins had shared some of his trips abroad. But when she'd fallen pregnant with Athena, he had been afraid that she would overtire herself. He had made changes, and she saw a great deal more of her handsome husband now and loved the fact.

In actuality this very day was the day of their second wedding anniversary, but in answer to all enquiries she had told everyone that no, they weren't doing anything special. That was a complete lie. Some things, however, weren't for sharing. Some celebrations were of a more private nature. She adjusted the narrow pearl shoulder straps on her short swirling green organza dress and set off for the tower.

She walked down the woodland path and saw him through the trees. Her steps quickened without her even being aware of the fact. The romantic scene of luxurious quilts, cushions and a marble table overflowing with tasty food was every bit as beautiful as she recalled, and her sunny smile broke out. Alexandros, lounging back against the cushions with a glass of wine cradled in one lean brown hand, began to get up.

'Don't move,' Katie urged softly. 'You look like a Roman emperor.'

'Bring on my dancing girls.'

'There's just me…will I do?'

Alexandros ran smouldering golden eyes over her and extended his hand. 'I like the dress… I like you in it, but I'll like you even more out of it, *agape mou*,' he confided, with the earthy honesty that was so much a part of him

In response, Katie shimmied her slight shoulders and swung her hips. With one lingering glance he could make her feel like the most beautiful, sexy woman alive. 'You are so predictable, Mr Christakis.'

Laughing, his lean strong face alive with humour and a powerful look of tenderness, Alexandros tugged her down beside him with possessive hands. He settled her back against the cushions and extracted a lingering kiss. 'Isn't it great to know we've had less than three years together and there's hopefully another forty-seven at least ahead of us?'

Touched by that reference to his grandparents' lifelong happiness as a couple, Katie told him how much she loved him. He reciprocated with fervour, and the drowsy heat of the afternoon passed while they reaffirmed their joy in having found each other.

HARLEQUIN *Presents*

Dinner at 8

Wined, dined and swept away by a British billionaire!

He's suave and sophisticated.
He's undeniably charming.
And above all, he treats her like a lady....

But don't be fooled....

Beneath the tux, there's a primal passionate lover,
who's determined to make her his!

In
THE CHRISTMAS BRIDE
by Penny Jordan...

Silas Stanway is furious! How did he end up playing
escort to some woman called Tilly and attending
a Christmas wedding in Spain? Silas thinks Tilly is
desperate, but he's in for a surprise....

**On sale December.
Buy your copy today!**

www.eHarlequin.com   HPDAE1206